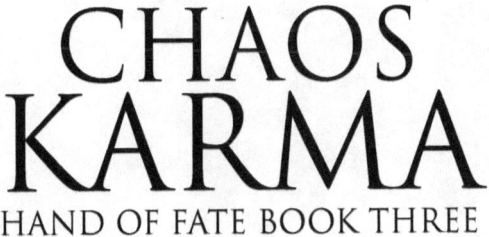

CHAOS
KARMA
HAND OF FATE BOOK THREE

CHAOS
KARMA
HAND OF FATE BOOK THREE

SHARON JOSS

AJA PUBLISHING
USA

Also by Sharon Joss

CHAPTER 1

THE SMELL OF chili and bacon grease hit me hard as I stepped inside the twenty-four hour diner on Third Street. Dave's Killer Burgers is practically an institution in Shore Haven. When I was a kid, the place used to be called Ed's Drive-In, but when Melvin Moody bought it twenty-some years ago, he converted it to a regular restaurant and renamed it for his pets— an ever-hungry school of Indigo Diamond piranhas as big as turkey platters. Dave's was probably the only restaurant in upstate New York with a floor-to-ceiling aquarium in the dining room.

Tourists come from miles around to see Mel feed his fish, but they keep coming back for the food. Mel told me once he learned how to cook in the Army, and maybe it's true, but put a spatula in his hand and fryer in arms reach and he's a magician. He's got more than fifty different burgers on the menu.

No fish sandwiches, though.

The front of the 50's-style diner is a glass-walled

patio with a roll-back roof so that in the summer, diners can eat outside. Inside, there is a front room with booths and a big U-shaped counter. The booths are all red tuck-and-roll vinyl, with plenty of chrome around the table and counter edges and a big ol' Wurlitzer jukebox by the front door. The cash register sits in the middle of the restaurant, dividing the brightly-lit front counter area from the darker dining room in the back, where it's all tables and chairs for bigger parties. The killer fish aquarium covers most of the back wall of the restaurant dining room.

Two sets of swinging doors lead into the kitchen. The one on the back wall is the 'in' door, and the one near the front counter is the 'out' door, and Mel is quick to fire any waitress or busboy that mixes them up. I started out bussing tables here in high school, and worked my way up to waitress until I got hired on as a parking control officer for the city of Pictson.

Mel and I go way back.

I passed through the 'in' doors into the kitchen, making my way past the dishwasher, soup kettles, and the pick-up station; around the far corner to the tiny windowless office where Mel was doing the books. He looked up only when I cleared my throat.

He slid the greasy paper cap off his head and ran his fingers through his hair. "What the hell are you doing here, Blackman? You get fired again?"

Mel is an Elvis man, through and through. If

I had to guess, I'd bet he's in his mid-to-late-fifties. His hair is thinner than it used to be, and the Grecian Formula he uses gives it an unnatural bronzy-greenish hue. He still wears it slicked back and shiny with Brylcreem. His office smelled like fryer grease and Aqua Velva aftershave. Today, like every day, he wore black-and-white checked pants and a grease-and-chili-stained white chef's jacket.

"No." But I could feel my cheeks burning. "Why do you always just assume that's why I'm here?"

He glared at me over his little half glasses. "Don't play games with me, girl. I'm busy. What do you want?"

Dark circles beneath his eyes warned me he hadn't been sleeping well—which I suppose explained his lack of friendly banter. "I just need a little extra cash."

"So I heard." He turned back to his books. "Why don't you just put in for overtime?"

Of course he had to know about the cutbacks. All the Picston cops ate at Dave's. "Okay, yes. They cut back my hours. I'm down to three days a week. My apartment burned up and I'm staying with a friend until I can afford to get my own place. You happy now?"

"Where you staying?

I debated telling him, but knowing Mel, he already knew the answer. It wasn't just cops that ate a Dave's, all the locals did. As a result, he usually had his finger on the pulse of everything going on in Shore

3

Haven. "The Coumlie house—just until I can get back on my feet." I still felt weird about explaining my living arrangement or admitting to people that I was related to her. "It belongs to my um, cousin now. Henri."

He scowled and shook his head. Mel had lived in Shore Haven for years, but like everybody else in town, he thought Madame Coumlie, the Hand of Fate and oh by the way my great-grandmother, was nothing but a fortune-teller. But she'd also been the direct descendant of Morta, one of the original three Fates. When she died, her legacy came to me.

"You been getting some bad publicity lately." He rubbed the stubble along his chin. "Might be bad for business."

Normally, Mel's teasing didn't bother me, and he could take it was well as he dished it. We both knew he'd give me the job. If I wasn't so desperate to get my life back to normal, I wouldn't have to beg. Living with Henri was about the last place on the planet I wanted to call home. I mean, I liked Henri, and giving me and my *djemon*, Blix, a place to stay in exchange for me tutoring him on how to pass as human was working out well, but I didn't have much privacy. My brand-new boyfriend, Rhys Warrick didn't seem to mind, *but I did*. I *needed* my own place.

"Come on, Mel, gimme a break. I'll even clean the fish tank. I noticed it's looking a little murky today." Mel always said I did a better job cleaning the tank than anyone. For some reason, the fish didn't get as stressed when I did the job. For all their bad-ass reputation, piranhas are actually quite delicate and difficult to care for.

He pushed the little half-glasses to the top of his head and leaned back in his chair, facing me. "No can do, Mattie. The day shift is full, and those girls all have seniority. All I've got is Thursday, Friday and Saturday graveyard."

Rats. Weekend graveyard shift was the worst. Eleven at night until seven in the morning. Nothing but drunks and sidework. Busy as hell, lousy tips, and three hours of cleaning the place before the morning shift came in. I'd be working Monday, Wednesday, and Friday on parking patrol, so Fridays would kick my ass.

And then there was the Spirit Festival to consider. As the new Hand of Fate, I'd agreed to be the Grand Marshal of the parade and Guest of Honor at the Spirit Ball. The parade wouldn't be a problem. I'd just have to sneak out of the Spirit Ball on Saturday before my shift started.

"Okay, I'll take it."

"Hold your horses, girlie. You're gonna have to wear the uniform. We got new ones last month—just for the graveyard girls."

"Well, it's about time." For as long as I could remember, the uniforms at Dave's had been circa 1950's soda jerk outfits. Waitresses wore a white blouse with a red and white pinstripe poodle skirt; the busboys wore white shirts with red bowties and black pants. I couldn't wait to see the new duds.

He opened one of the metal lockers against the back wall and pulled out a purple plastic hangar with a few stray wisps of black cloth pinned to it. I winced inwardly as he held it up. "Made locally, so I got a good discount. If it fits, you've got the job."

I fingered the sheer fabric, trying to sort out the costume. It was not much more than a tissue-thin black silk bustier cinched over ruffled black panties and fishnet tights. More appropriate for lingerie. A teensy black ruffled apron, with a cheapy plastic sword hung from a sash at the waist. A black eye patch hung from the neck of the hanger. "What the hell, Mel? Are you serious?"

He grinned. "I'm doing you a favor, Blackman. The graveyard girls tell me their tips have tripled, and business has shot through the roof since we changed the uniforms. You still want the job?"

CHAPTER 2

IN SHORE HAVEN, the undead come out after midnight. So do the paranorms and the Alternate Individuals, or AIs, as they like to call themselves. People like Henri, my landlord. They come to Dave's Killer Burgers to do business and socialize. It's the only 24-hour business in town, and one of the few places where the AI's feel comfortable mingling with humans.

Humans came to Dave's after the bars closed, and there were a double fistful of bars in Shore Haven.

Mel hadn't lied. Graveyard shift was a lot busier than I remembered. And the costumes the other girls wore, while equally skimpy, were all slightly different. There was a frilly a cowgirl, a devil, a superhero—all wearing the same basic costume as me, but with a different cheesy prop. I told Mel I couldn't see with the eye patch on, but he wouldn't listen, so I wore it flipped up except when he was around. I swallowed my pride every time I picked up my tip, but the money was good.

My only solace was in knowing that Rhys would never see me in the pirate get-up. He'd left for Scotland a couple weeks earlier to close out his personal affairs. We'd made plans to get a place together when he came back. In the meantime, I was going to work my ruffled ass off and save every penny I could.

It was just after two in the morning and I was in the middle of the Saturday night bar rush when I got an emergency page. Before he left, Rhys had set up his phone to forward his calls to me. We weren't supposed to use our cell phones on duty, but it was an old friend, Lou Scali.

Lou was an ex-cop who'd taken early retirement in the latest round of City cutbacks and opened his own private detective agency. So private, he only worked word of mouth. Lou's clients were all connected to the paranormal community trusted Lou because he was one of their own.

He wanted me to meet him immediately at the motor court next to the amusement park.

I stepped into the walk-in refrigerator for privacy. "I can't, I'm working. I don't get off until seven."

"This can't wait that long, Mattie. Normally I'd call Rhys, and let him take a look before calling the feds, but he's not here."

Rhys Warrick is a visiting professor at University of Rochester, specializing in ancient cultures. He's the first guy the feds and local authorities go to for answers when they're looking at a suspected paranormal crime scene. What's not generally known is that he's also an immortal djenie more than two thousand years old, so a lot of his expertise comes from first-hand knowledge. He was the one who discovered I was heir to the Hand of Fate and started this whole shebang.

And by the way, coolest boyfriend *ever*.

But I'm not Rhys. "What do you expect me to do? What is it?"

"It's complicated. There are other people involved. People who can't afford to be involved. Hell, *I* can't afford to be involved. Look, I'm serious, I need you out here. This is Hand of Fate business, I think."

That meant *djemons*. Great. Goosebumps raced up my arms, or maybe it was the refrigerated air in the walk-in. The last demon I faced just about killed me. I wasn't in any hurry to repeat the experience.

Lou must've sensed my reluctance. "If not you, Mattie, who?"

Whatever it was, it had Lou rattled. I was still new to this whole Hand of Fate stuff, but I swore an oath to the goddess Morta that I'd serve and protect her subjects, and Lou was one of them. "Oh all right. I'll tell LaRue I'm sick. I can't come right now, we're too busy." LaRue was the lead waitress and manager on graveyard shift. "Give me an hour."

Fifty minutes later, I pulled into the parking lot of the Shore Happy Motor Court—a collection of dreary rundown cabins on the far side of Heavenly Shores Amusement Park. There had been a rainstorm a couple hours earlier, and the still air and humidity was miserable. In upstate New York, July is the sweatiest month of the year.

I spotted Lou when he stepped out from behind the dumpster to greet me. Even in the dimly lit parking lot, he's easy to recognize. He's a little guy, shorter than me even, with a thin dark comb-over, sad eyes, and a perpetually mournful expression. And unlike some cops I could think of, he's not a dick. Hell, I like Lou.

Even though I don't know what he is, exactly.

As the living incarnation of the Queen of Death, I think I'm supposed to, but I don't. He's got no lifeline. No aura. Nada. He's not alive, but not dead either. It's hardly the kind of thing I could come out and ask without being rude. Whatever he is, he's one of mine. Mine to serve and protect.

His eyes went wide at the sight of my ruffled floozy pirate outfit, and I blushed. "Took you long enough."

At least he knew better than to make a crack. "What's so important?"

"A body."

A little thrill ran through me. Suddenly, I was

wide awake. "Seriously?"

"This way." Lou led the way past the dumpster, down the cracked and broken concrete walkway toward the last cabin in the park.

To call them cabins is overly generous. Seventy or eighty years ago, they were vacation rentals for urban refugees escaping the sweltering summer heat. Half a century ago, they served as employee housing for the amusement park workers. When I was a kid, these places rented by the hour, and I'd wait outside while my mother made friends and 'entertained' her clients. Now, these filthy, ramshackle sheds were home to vagrants, drug users, and people who had no other place to go.

Light gleamed around the splintered frame of the cottage at the end of the row. As Lou eased the door open, I noticed he was wearing gloves. I rubbed my hands on my, um, ruffles. "Shouldn't I be wearing gloves, too?"

He shook his head. "Nah. Just don't touch anything." He pushed the door open and stood aside. "After you."

I clasped my hands together in front of me to keep them out of trouble and squeezed past him through the doorway. My attention was immediately drawn to the brown, naked form lying on the bed.

A mummy?

The body was nothing more than mahogany-colored skin stretched taut over a skeleton. Lying on his side, his knees drawn up to his chest, his head thrown back. His long stringy hair was completely white. His eyes were gone; the lids had sunk deep into his skull. His lips had shrunk away from his teeth in a ghastly grimace. I'd seen dead bodies before, but not like this. He looked like one of those petrified people they pulled out of peat bogs in Ireland.

A rumble sounded from behind me.

Lou rubbed his stomach. "Sorry, I haven't eaten since lunch, and you smell like chili fries."

I snorted. "Hello, I just got off work. I wasn't expecting to be called out to, um, this." I inspected the body. Come to think of it, there was no smell of decay in the room. Except for dank smell of the room itself, there was no smell of any kind. "Who is he?"

Lou stepped closer to the bed. "His name is William Parry. He's the mayor's cousin. Lead singer for Wiley Willy and the Rogues."

I knew him. I bent over the desiccated corpse, trying to discern Willy's features, but nothing looked familiar. Everybody in Shore Haven knew Wiley Willy and the Rogues. They played outdoor concerts every summer at the amusement park. Also weddings, beach parties, bar mitzvahs, and they were the official band of the Spirit Festival. They'd been around for years. Willy was probably in his late thirties, but this man looked decades older.

"How can you be sure?"

Lou picked up a wallet lying on the dust-covered nightstand and showed me the man's driver's license. "Because I've been following him for the last few days. Let's just say Mayor Brunson asked me to keep an eye on him. Willy's behavior has been erratic lately. Brunson thought maybe he was into to something he shouldn't be. I followed him here just before midnight. I figured maybe he was meeting someone, right? No one came in, and no one left. I finally got curious, and decided to check on him. When he wouldn't answer my knock, I had to force the door. Found him like this."

"Where are his clothes?

"I've no idea. I looked everywhere. There's a closet full of spider webs, if you don't believe me."

I scowled. "You're saying he walked in here stark naked a few hours ago and ended up like this? That's not possible."

"Well, he wasn't naked when he got here, sister. That's why I thought I'd give you a crack at it before I called it in." He flashed me the cash inside the wallet. A thick wad of fifties. "Whoever did this wasn't in it for the money."

Not for the first time, I wished Rhys hadn't gone back to Scotland. He probably could have told us what happened here in about two minutes. Instinctively, I reached out to the leathery corpse, letting my fingers hover just over the surface of the skin. I opened that part of my mind which linked me to my ancestor, the

Goddess of Death, but got nothing. No body heat here. No aura, no lifeline.

Lou tapped his gloved finger against the skin. The skin was hard and stretched tight and hard as a tambourine.

"Roll him over," I said. "Let's see if he has any marks on the other side."

In his stiffened, dehydrated state, Lou flipped the body over with as much apparent effort as flipping over an empty pizza box.

I leaned in close, looking for any marks, but found nothing. "Was he human?"

Lou shrugged. "Possibly. The mayor is a registered paranormal, but maybe Willy-boy here was unregistered. Brunson could tell you."

I made a face. "Tell me what? Why is this *my* problem?"

"Because once I call in the feds, I'm out of this. They'll be all over Brunson; monitoring his cell phone activity. I won't be able to get anywhere near him without attracting unwanted attention. Attention I don't want or need. That new FBI agent, Roper and his damn demon-sniffing dog, for example."

Roper and his *djemon*-dog Jager were the least of my worries, but they had the entire AI community on high alert.

"And I can?" I couldn't keep my eyes off the ghastly expression on Wiley Willy's face. Was it agony or ecstasy? Hard to tell.

"Sure, you work in the same building. You're the guest of honor and Grand Marshal of the Festival. Nobody will think twice about you talking to the Mayor. Especially since now you're probably gonna need a new band for the Spirit Ball."

"What?" Lou was moving a little too fast for me. I still wasn't certain that this bit of jerky was Wiley Willy.

"The drummer, Kid Harsh, was found dead by the side of the Throughway two weeks ago. Based on the desiccated condition of the body, the coroner couldn't determine the cause of death, but concluded he'd been hit by a truck and probably been dead for weeks before someone discovered the body. Now I'm not so sure."

Road kill. I shivered in the stuffy room. "And you're certain you saw him walking around a few hours ago."

"I wouldn't lie to the Hand of Fate."

"And now he's a frickin' raisin."

CHAPTER 3

THE CASSOWEGO SPIRITUALIST Camp is a former summer resort situated on sixty wooded acres twelve miles east of Shore Haven. Established in 1907, it's listed on the New York Historical Register. There are about 35 of the original cabins still standing, and another 60 newer cabins, built in the swingin' sixties. It was originally set up as a non-traditional religious retreat, but the current residents are all paranormals, although many are unregistered. They've been living and doing whatever they do in harmony for more than a century. About 20 of the residents are mediums who offer counseling from their homes. The International Spirit Festival had its roots here—it developed from the annual camp meetings in the 1930's.

The morning sun was already shining above the treetops when I stopped at the front gate and pushed the button on the intercom. "Welcome to the spiritual heart of New York," the disembodied voice droned.

"Please state your name and the purpose of your visit."

"Mattie Blackman here for Madame Parry." I hadn't wanted to come, but Mayor Brunson didn't want his aunt Marjorie to get the news about her son over the phone or from the feds. "Jim Brunson sent me."

Lou called in the tip about Wiley Willy anonymously, so the mayor's office wouldn't be directly involved. That way, the Feds would be more likely to start looking for the real killer, rather than looking for skeletons in the mayor's not-exactly-human personal life.

"Just tell her what you told me," Brunson instructed me. "Aunt Marjorie is a medium. She'll know the truth in your words, and maybe she'll even be able to tell you something about what happened to Willy. She can help you find his killer."

I didn't have the heart to say no.

The light on the top of the intercom turned green, and the ornate, wrought-iron gate slowly opened before me. I goosed the gas in my trusty Honda, and followed the rutted road as it wound through the groves of maple, pine, and birch.

Fourth house on the right, Brunson had told me. The term 'house' was a generous one. Based on the architecture, the tiny turquoise structure looked more like a garden shed, to me. Must've been one of the original cabins.

Aunt Marjorie, dressed in a blue plaid flannel

robe, was waiting for me on the porch. I guessed her to be in her late fifties. She wore her dark hair, shot through with silver, pulled back into a tight ponytail. Broad cheekbones and olive skin gave her a decidedly exotic look that was handsome, rather than pretty. Hard blue eyes drilled into me like cold steel as I stepped out of the car. Once she got a good look at me, her mouth thinned to a disapproving line.

More than anything I wished I was wearing something other than Mel's ridiculous tacky pirate costume. I couldn't even get rid of the stupid plastic sword, because it was glued to the apron, and without the apron, I was just a girl in frilly black panties, fishnet stockings, and a bustier.

"You didn't have to come. I know William is dead. I felt him go."

I stood on the porch, my hand glued to the railing. Her aura pulsed with the same odd blue-green-black that Mayor Brunson's did. I wondered if it was because they were family or because they shared the same paranormal profile. Probably both.

"I'm so sorry for your loss, Mrs. Parry. Mayor Brunson asked me to bring you the news. He didn't want the feds to be the ones to tell you."

A ghost of a smile softened her expression. "Jimmy was always a good boy." She inclined her head toward the front door of her cabin. "Come inside. I must speak to you."

The one-room cabin gave me her whole life's story at a glance. To the left of the front door, her reading table sat below the window, where a hand-painted 'OPEN' sign hung from the upper sash. In front of the window, a simple round painted table sat with two wooden chairs, the obligatory crystal ball centered on the tabletop. The right side of the room was set up as a kitchen, around a soapstone sink with an old-fashioned pump-handled copper faucet. An open corner cupboard held cups and dishes, and the wood-burning stove squatted like a toad in the center of the room, its pipe vented through the peaked roof overhead. Next to it, a tiny table held an old, pedal-operated sewing machine—Brunson told me his aunt earned extra money sewing decorative banners of nylon and canvas. Next to it, brightly-colored pieces of fabric were draped over the back of a gun-metal grey folding metal chair. In the back third of the room, partially screened by a gauzy veil, a mattress slumped on the floor against the back wall, cradling limp but brightly-colored pillows in one corner. Opposite, a narrow bunk sat empty, but for a bare mattress. The morning sun had not yet reached the shaded clearing; the cabin was lit only by oil lanterns and lit candles. The walls were plastered with photographs—I recognized Mayor Brunson as a boy in several—arm-in-arm with a younger boy, the future Wiley William, I presumed. The family resemblance was hard to miss.

She motioned me to sit—the intensity of her expression made it an order I chose not to question. I took a seat at her reading table. She didn't seem all that upset about losing her son. When she spoke, her voice was strong.

"Where in hell did you get *that* costume?"

I felt the heat rise in my face, and not just from embarrassment. *Really? Your son is dead and you want to lecture me about what I'm wearing?* My sympathy for her cooled considerably. I ignored the question. "He was found at the motor lodge next to the amusement park. Do you have any idea what he was doing there?"

"Neldene's been designing for the Festival for decades. Her taste is impeccable. She would never dress you or any woman in something like--."

I cut her off. "Listen to me! I'm trying to talk to you about your son."

She stared at me as if I was the one who as nuts. I took a deep breath and tried again. "It was an unnatural death. We won't know exactly how he died until the coroner finishes his investigation, but I saw the body. I've never seen anything like it—don't you care about what happened to him?"

"I said where did you get that costume?" She reached across the table and put her hand on my arm. "Oh." Her eyes stared off into the distance as her fingers gripped my wrist. A line of spittle leaked from the corner of her mouth.

I frowned. Her hands were ice-cold. A sheen of sweat gleamed on her forehead. Her aura began to fade. There was something seriously wrong with her. "Are you all right, Mrs. Parry? Shall I call someone?"

She shivered and seemed to come out of it. Her blue eyes once again bored into mine. "Listen to me, you stupid girl. I knew he was in danger from the beginning. I tried to warn him, but he wouldn't listen. Always too trusting, that boy. I mourned William's passing for six months before he died. My tears were spent months ago—I felt only peace when he finally went. Have you any idea how it is for a mother to lose a child? Even a grown child. It should never happen. No one would listen to me." She grabbed my hand again, and her voice dropped to a deeper register. "I told Jimmy, and I'll tell you. You've got to trust the vampires, lest you suffer the same fate, child."

Adrenaline shot through me. "Vampires?" Lou and I had checked the body for bite marks—we hadn't found any. The only vamp I knew of, Enrique, had run against Jim Brunson in the last election and lost. There were rumors he'd been the one behind a whisper campaign which ultimately forced Brunson to come out as a Paranormal. Fortunately for Brunson, the plan backfired and didn't hurt his popularity much—he won anyway. Odd that Marjorie would be on their side, though.

"They will not do you wrong. Stop this thing before the Spirit Ball or we all die."

Her eyes rolled back in her head and she slumped over in her chair.

"What! What thing? Mrs. Parry!" Panicked, I jumped up to feel her pulse, even as the light of her aura went out. Madame Marjorie was dead.

Sheriff Reynolds arrived in minutes, just before the ambulance. I waited for him out on the porch, just as Madame Marjorie had waited for me, and then followed him inside. He checked her pulse and lifted her eyelids. He nodded once, and then scowled when he noticed my outfit. "What happened here?"

I silently cursed Mel for the hundredth time for making me wear this damn thing. "I was just talking to her and she keeled over." Outside, the siren announced the coming of the ambulance.

His scowl deepened. "What were you talking about?"

I felt the heat rise in my face. See, I've known Sheriff Reynolds nearly all my life. He's got a reputation as straight shooter and an ace lawman, but I don't think he really sees me as a fellow officer, even though, arguably, parking control is part of the Picston Police Department. I think his opinion of me has been forever tainted by that time he arrested me for murder. The real murderer ended up being somebody else, but I don't think it mattered to him. He's the kind of lawman who wouldn't forget about something like that. I'm pretty sure he still holds it against me.

And he's smart. The last time he interrogated me, I lied through my teeth, and I'm pretty sure he knew it, because he was already looking at me as if I was going to lie to him again. His cynical expression made that pretty clear.

If Wiley Willy's body hadn't been found yet, it soon would be. If I told the sheriff I was here to inform Marjorie of her son's death, he'd want to know how I knew. I'd be opening a huge can of worms—not just for me, but for Lou Scali and Mayor Brunson—something to be avoided at all costs. The Sheriff's department had jurisdiction over Shore Haven, so the corpse lying on the bed at the motor lodge belonged to him. Once Willy's body was found, Reynolds would immediately make the connection. He might have even been on route to tell her about her son's death himself. Yeah, chances were better than good he already knew about the recent demise of Wiley Willy.

Obviously, I had to lie. Besides, he was expecting it. Something innocent and plausible, yet impossible for him to verify.

I took a deep breath. "I needed a dress for the Spirit Ball."

Three hours later, I was still in Sheriff Reynolds's interview room. They believed me about Marjorie—they'd *have* to let me go soon. It was pretty obvious that the poor woman had suffered some sort of heart failure or aneurism.

I could barely keep my eyes open, even after six cups of coffee. All I had to do was keep cool and not say anything stupid. Reynolds had asked every question four or five different ways, and my answers had been consistent. We both knew he had no reason to keep me.

There was a soft knock at the door, and Agent Roper came in, waving a clear plastic evidence bag. "We found this at the motor court. It was caught on a splinter in the broken door." His eyes never left my face.

Ted Roper is the new paranormal investigator assigned to the Monroe County FBI office. His dog, Jager, has been trained to alert on djemons. Oddly enough, Jager is a *djenie* dog—a *djemon* who was freed from servitude when his master died, and chose the form of a black dog when he transformed into a djenie. Whoever found Jager at the pound, didn't know the dog wasn't really a dog at all. Jager is aces at sniffing out *djemons*, but he's not mortal, so he answers to me above all others.

Agent Roper is generally thought of as a bit of a hard-ass. The AI community is pretty much terrified of him, but I think that's because nobody knows him or what he'll do. Monroe County is his first assignment as a paranormal investigator, and from what I hear, he's been more than a little frustrated that he hasn't found any illicit paranormal activity to investigate. Shore Haven is second only to New Orleans in terms of a registered paranormal population.

Roper tossed the evidence bag onto the desk. "There's your smoking gun on the William Parry murder, Sheriff."

Reynolds held up the bag for inspection and my heart skipped a beat.

Even from across the interview table, I could identify the bit of snagged black ruffle from my pirate uniform panties.

Suddenly, Sheriff Reynolds looked wide awake. "Well, well. What do we have here? Stand up, Mattie. Let's get a better look at that get-up you're almost wearing."

I smothered a groan and kept my hands on the desktop, my face expressionless. The jig was up. In two minutes or less, they'd know for certain I'd been inside Wiley Willy's room. I wasn't about to stand up and let them inspect my ruffled assets for clues.

I said what I should have said three hours earlier. "I want to speak to my attorney."

CHAPTER 4

I DON'T KNOW what strings Gerard Fontaigne pulled to get me out of there, and I had to give Sheriff Reynolds my waitress uniform as evidence, but I was on my way home four hours later. Reynolds impounded my ancient Honda, Trusty Rusty, to search for evidence, but it was almost worth walking out of the Sheriff's station wrapped in a blanket to see the look of frustration on his and Roper's faces.

Almost.

Fontaigne gave me a ride back to Shore Haven in his Bentley. I'd never been in such a posh car. The door panels were inlaid with gorgeous rosewood trim, smooth as satin. The leather upholstery was butter-soft. "Thanks for coming, Gerard. I really thought Reynolds was going to arrest me for murder. That gung-ho federal agent was pushing pretty hard."

Fontaigne had been my great-grandmother's attorney for decades. Not that she ever got arrested or anything—Gerard is a tax lawyer. But this isn't the first time he's dealt me a 'get out of jail' card.

"Think nothing of it, my dear. You should have called me earlier. I doubt you would have been charged with murder. After all the bad press the last time, Reynolds is too smart to arrest you for anything without solid evidence."

"That scrap of fabric from the ruffles on my uniform puts me at in the room with Willy Parry."

Fontaigne gave me a self-satisfied smile. "Ah, but Wiley Willy's death has not yet been classified as a homicide. And I suspect the coroner will have a difficult time determining Madame Marjorie's as well. Suspicious, yes. But murder..." he shrugged. "Charges for both cases, if they come, will be at the discretion of the District Attorney. For now, you are a person of interest."

I glanced at the speedometer. We were humming along the Throughway at 110mph with hardly a whisper; the ride so smooth, it felt like we were flying.

"They both died the same night, Gerard. That's more than suspicious, and I'm the common denominator. People have been convicted on a lot less."

Another non-committal shrug. His silver hair perfectly matched the exterior of the Bentley. Always impeccably groomed, a tiny blood-red rosebud peeked out of the lapel of his understated Italian suit.

"You are hardly common, Mattie. In the last few

years, the Spirit Festival has become a truly international event. Last year, it brought more money into Monroe County than the Lilac Festival and Clothesline Art Festival combined. I suspect the DA is going to be reluctant to press charges against the Grand Marshal of the Spirit Festival for failure to report a dead body. Certainly not *before* the festival--the international publicity would be disastrous. He'll do nothing until he has the coroner's findings."

Great. A sense of doom settled over me. Marjorie probably died of a heart attack, but Willy's death was definitely suspicious. I had no doubts at all that his cause of death would be supernatural in nature. People don't just die and get turned into mummies. And it was hard to understand how both of them died within hours of each other. Heck, I *knew* I hadn't done anything to either one of them and I felt guilty. Of course I would be the obvious suspect. The *only* suspect.

I wrapped the blanket more tightly around me. "What if the coroner's finding points to homicide? How long do you think I'll have to wait?" I couldn't help but feel that for every little step forward, I took three giant steps back. All I wanted was to earn a little extra cash working at Dave's, and now I was *a person of interest* in two suspicious deaths. I thought wistfully of Rhys, safe in Scotland, and belatedly wished I'd gone with him.

Fontaigne flipped on the right-hand blinker and braked for the Picston exit. The Bentley decelerated as gracefully as a falling star. "I'm afraid I cannot answer that. It takes a long as it takes. There is no statute of limitations for murder."

I hated that helpless feeling I used to get when my mother went off on a binge. She always came back, but it would be sick with worry for as many days and nights as it took until she came home. Or until we got the call that she'd been arrested. If she'd pulled something like that today, I would have gone after her and dragged her out of whatever hole she'd fallen into, but she'd committed suicide when I was in high school. I couldn't do anything about it then, but I was an adult now. It was me in that hole, and I felt completely helpless to do anything about it. *Crap*. I thrummed my fingers on the armrest.

Marjorie was a psychic. She'd said she knew her son was going to die for months. She must've talked to someone about it. Maybe Mayor Brunson knew something. And she'd mentioned vampires. I shuddered. Ugh. Maybe I could get Lou to talk to them. Lou and I made a good team. We'd figure out what happened to Wiley Willy in no time. Solve the murder—or at least the mystery of his death—and get me off the hook. Just the thought of investigating this case made me feeling better. I yawned. I couldn't wait to get started.

After a nap.

The nap didn't happen—at least not like I planned.

The nagging headache which had started in the wee hours of the morning had blossomed to mind-numbing proportions by the time Fontaigne dropped me off at Madame Coumlie's. Even though I was living at the house my great grandmother had lived in for close to a century, it was only temporary, and I felt funny calling it home. To my mind, home was where your clothes were in the closet, you knew where everything was, and your bed didn't smell like mothballs.

But beggars couldn't be choosers. I took a quick shower and surveyed the closet for something to wear. Even without the pirate uniform, my choices were limited. My underwear inventory was critically low. Only my day job uniform--a white shirt and navy culottes, three tee-shirts and one pair of jeans had survived the fire and ah, aftermath of my old apartment. I silently thanked Henri for doing the laundry, and got dressed.

I pulled the teapot full of bills and coins I'd been using as a tip jar out from under the bed and sat down to count out the money. A second uniform from Mel would probably set me back a hundred bucks—money I'd earmarked for a security deposit my own apartment. As I counted up the rolls of quarters, Blix crawled into my lap for a snuggle.

Blix is my baby *djemon*.

Oh I supposed 'baby' isn't exactly the right word for it. Once a creature of the ether, Blix became a fully materialized djemon when I named him. Now, he's with me until death do us part. He's still small, not much bigger than a kitten, but will grow in size with every command I give him.

Instinctively, my fingers went to his warm little belly. His rear legs kicked out as I tickled him, and his homely, wrinkled face split into a toothy grin. Blix loves being petted and tickled. He's grown a little since I first named him, and he's got itchy little nubs behind his shoulders where his wings are starting to bud. His hairless, charcoal-black form is that of a sphinx; I'm guessing that he'll need to get a lot bigger before he sprouts wings and feathers. I like him small and cuddly like this. At this size, he's easy to hide and doesn't smell or eat or poop—he's the perfect pet.

But there's the rub. If I don't give him commands, he can't grow. A djemon which doesn't grow will be left defenseless when his master dies and he becomes a djenie. Small djenies cannot transform into human form and are more easily killed. And if I do give him enough commands so that he can grow, but don't educate him, he'll be unprepared to live on his own in human form after I die. And Henri told me I can't just send him into the ether until I need him, because learning to live among earth-bound mortals is a huge part of his education. Most people don't realize that being a demon master is a big responsibility—and that's only one of my new roles as the Hand of Fate. I didn't ask for the job, but I gave my word, and when you make an oath to the Goddess of Death, that's one promise you *don't* want to break.

I headed downstairs for a bit of pre-nap foraging, my heart set on a thick slice of Henri's French toast. It was the first thing I taught him how to make, and he was already better at it than me. Henri's version was a heavenly concoction made from thick-sliced cinnamon bread filled with sliced strawberries and cream cheese; topped with whipped cream and drizzled with warm strawberry syrup. Mmmm.

Henri was in what used to be my great-grandmother's dining room, practicing the stylized movements of his Qhua Bei exercises. Henri had been Madame Coumlie's djemon before she died—a sphinx, just like Blix only pony-sized. When she died, he transformed into human form.

Henri is a djenie—like Rhys. After his transformation, Rhys introduced him to his Qhua Bei Master, Foo. Qhua Bei was no martial art I'd ever heard of before but Rhys told me he'd been studying it for centuries, and it was not so much as a self-defense practice as a way of life. For Henri, the time he spent with Master Foo was the high point of his week. One of the first things he did after Madame Coumlie left the house to him in her will was to rip out the carpeting and lay down padded rubber mats in the dining room, turning it into his practice room and meditation studio.

Henri moved deliberately through his forms, his face intent, his attention focused on his movements. Still new to his human form, the exercises gave him focus and helped him adjust to life in the world beyond the ether. In the few weeks since he'd begun practicing with Master Foo, his gaunt form had developed into a slim, wiry physique. Like a long-distance runner or an acrobat, Henri was flexible and strong without the hard muscle bulk Rhys had acquired over the last two millennia.

The physicality of Qhua Bei practice was only one side of the discipline. The meditative aspect of the practice was of equal importance, and Henri seemed to be thriving on both aspects. When Rhys left, Master Foo had taken Rhys's place as a mentor to Henri. Henri would go to Master Foo's studio every day if the old man would allow it. With my schedule, I could only manage once a week.

I could hear the music blasting through his earbuds from across the room. Once they have a master, djemons only hear their master's commands. Since becoming a djenie, Henri has become absolutely mad for music. He's got those earbuds plugged in just about every time I see him. Henri looks to be in his late twenties, but in a lot of ways, he reminds me of

34

a teen-ager. He's eager to experience new sensations, and explore his independence and quickly immerses himself into each new passion. Without Rhys to guide him, it was Master Foo who cautioned him to cut back on his practice regime, to eat the proper foods, and to give his body time to rest.

Henri finally noticed me standing in the doorway and popped out the buds. "Oh good, you're ready. Let's go. We're going to be late. I don't want to keep Master Foo waiting."

My heart sank. There went breakfast *and* the nap. Before Rhys left for Scotland, he'd made me promise to study with Master Foo and learn the basics of Qhua Bei self defense. After getting abducted by that soul-stealing Papa Shango, I had to admit that it was probably a good idea.

But my feelings about the practice of Qhua Bei and master Foo in particular were pretty much the exact opposite of Rhys and Henri. Henri was far better at it than I, and working two jobs, I couldn't seem to find the time to practice. But the worst part was the meditation. It put me right to sleep. Every time.

If there was one thing Master Foo did not tolerate, it was sleeping during meditation time. Not one little bit.

Fortunately, the session was only an hour. Maybe I could get a nap in before I told Mel I needed a new uniform.

The Qhua Bei studio was just two blocks away, so

we were there in minutes. Master Foo's house looks like nothing from the street—just a brown shingled cottage with neat white trim. His studio, which is reached by the alley running behind the house, was built much like some ancient Asian temple. Thick beams support a pagoda-like roof structure, and sliding translucent panels divide up the studio into two areas—one for private meditation, and one for his students.

Thwhack!

I winced as the bamboo slats hit the bottom of my bare feet, yanking me out of the deep sleep I'd tried my best to avoid. I blushed and looked over at Henri, who lay there with the barest hint of a smile at the corners of his mouth.

Master Foo waggled his finger at me. "Again, Missy."

I closed my eyes again. I *hate* meditation. *Exhale. Empty your lungs until they are merely flaccid balloons lying limp within your rib cage. Force out the rest of your wasted breath even further. Out with it, until there is nothing left and push a little bit beyond. Rest within the empty place and build up the need to fill it.*

Inhale. Breathe deep. Fill your lungs from the bottom up; allow the life and light and peace to fill your soul. Up to the very top of your capacity and beyond. Rest within the fullness and allow the breath of life to expand beyond your earthly and physical constraints.

Thwhack! "Again, Missy."

I jumped. Adrenaline and guilt surged through me. *Dang, that smarts.* I fought to stay awake. These late night shifts at work were killing me. As I concentrated on my breathing, I thought about Rhys and wished he'd call. Before he left he told me he wasn't sure about internet or cell phone coverage in Scotland and not to worry if I didn't hear from him. Easy for him to say. I hadn't even gotten so much as a text message from him. The only text I'd gotten lately had been from Lou Scali. I thought about Wiley Willy's desiccated corpse.

Thwhack!

Sheesh that hurts.

Master Foo tapped me in the center of my chest with this bamboo instrument of torture. "Do not think, simply be. Focus on breath. Again, Missy."

I hate meditation.

CHAPTER 5

I DON'T WORK on Sunday nights, but the fish tank had to be cleaned, so I went to see Mel after my lesson with Master Foo. Henri came with me, because, well, *piranhas*. And I told him he could help.

Mel had the door to his office closed, and that meant he either had the safe open inside or he was on the phone. Either way, no one dared to knock on Mel's door when it was closed.

Business is slow enough on Sunday afternoons that the hostess doesn't usually seat anyone in the back dining room where the piranha tank is. I got Henri to help me pull the black drapes across the front glass. Hard as it is to believe, piranhas are timid, shy fish. They can easily get over-stimulated, especially by movement or noise, and die or start attacking each other. So whenever the dining room was being vacuumed or for the weekly tank cleaning, the black-out drapes are used to minimize visual stimulation.

Cleaning out the piranha tank twice a week for Mel was the first job I ever had, and over the years I've cleaned it more than anyone except for Mel. He's got thirty of the largest and most aggressive piranhas known—Indigo Diamonds, they're called in the trade. Big as turkey platters with vicious-looking tricuspid teeth. Dangerous, yes, but I think they're beautiful—black and silver with blue-purple neon stripes along their bellies.

Since they're meat eaters, and sloppy feeders, it's essential that the water in the tank be kept clean. Most of the kitchen staff are understandably reluctant to do it. Either that, or they do a piss-poor job because they're afraid of the fish.

The tank is topped by a heavy lid—Mel had a folding door-type cover rigged up, because piranhas are incredible jumpers. After a third of the water had been drained from the tank, I folded back half of the lid, used the ladder to crawl up onto it, and went to work.

Lying on the folded back lid, I stretched as far as I could reach; my arms completely submerged in the water while I scrubbed the glass and then ran the water vac across the gravel on the bottom. I knew to take my time and not make quick movements, which tend to aggravate the fish. The piranhas seemed happy enough to play peek-a-boo at me from behind a big rock formation in the furthest corner of the six-foot tall by eight-foot wide custom-built tank.

I pointed to the long-handled scrubber utensil

I used to scrape algae off the inside of the glass. "Hand me that, please." It was the only way to remove the algae all the way down to the bottom of the glass without actually getting into the aquarium, and even I wasn't that brave.

Henri passed it up to me. "Aren't you worried they'll attack?"

"Nope." They could shred the meat off my arm in seconds, if they wanted to, but they don't. "They let me know if I'm moving too fast by grunting."

"I didn't think fish could vocalize."

"Piranhas can." I moved the scrubber toward the huddled group hiding in the corner. Immediately, a staccato of thumps sounded from the group and they immediately grew more agitated. I withdrew the scrubber from the tank to give them time to settle down. "If you know what you're doing, there's nothing to worry about."

After they settled down again, I finished the job and began refilling the tank. They came out of the corner as soon as I climbed down from the ladder. I slowly drew aside the drapes.

"Look how happy they are," Henri said.

I wiped my arms dry with a clean towel. The fish did appear to enjoy swimming through the stream of freshly filtered water flowing into their tank. I shut the folding door panel across the top of the tank and slipped the locking bolts into place for safety.

"They know her scent in the water. They know she won't hurt them." Mel observed. He'd come up behind us. "People underestimate fish, but they can recognize faces and voices."

It's true. The only time Mel spoke in low tones was around the fish. They were his babies. Sometimes, if no one was around, I'd hear him talking to them.

Sure enough, the school clustered animatedly at the glass, their unblinking silvery eyes fixed on Mel.

He looked beat, but I couldn't wait any longer. "I need a new uniform."

"What the hell, Mattie?"

Immediately, the fish began to dart around the tank in jerky motions. A danger sign. Mel jerked his head toward the office and I followed meekly, waiting for the lecture I knew was coming.

He slumped into his office chair, looking more tired than I'd ever seen him. The guy never took a day off. "What is it this time? Lost at the laundromat or burned up in a fire?"

"Hey, neither of those times was my fault." No reason to tell him the whole story, though. "I snagged it. The fabric is so cheap, it shredded like tissue paper. I can't wear it. I'm not kidding, Mel. I need a new one."

From the look he gave me, I knew he didn't believe a word. "A whole new uniform." He shook his head. "I told you it was the last one I had." He waggled his finger at me. "And if you think you're going to show up Thursday night without a uniform, don't bother. You'll have to buy your own this time. And if I were you, I wouldn't say the word 'cheap' around her."

"Around who?"

"Felicity Caprice. She runs the dress shop just down the block."

By Monday, the news was out that Wiley Willy had been found dead under suspicious circumstances, but the coroner had not yet released the cause of death. The paper said only that the investigation was continuing, and witnesses were being interviewed. His mother's death was described as a "collapse", suffered after the shock of hearing about her son's death. Anyone with information about the case...blah, blah, blah.

I don't know how Gerard Fontaigne managed to keep the details or my name out of it, but I kept to myself at work that day. I had to take the bus to work because my car was still sitting in an impound lot over in Webster. I had the feeling a big bad cloud of shitstorm was about to hit, and the last thing I wanted to do was to go buy a new cheesy sleazy uniform I knew I was going to hate to replace the previous cheesy sleazy uniform that got me into this whole mess.

Les Belles Jolie dress shop was just three doors

down from Dave's Killer Burgers. It's one of those places that people walk by a million times and never go into. At least not me. And I'd never seen anyone else go in there, either. Based on the way Mel said her name, with an odd and throaty kind of yearning, I figured that ol' Mel might actually have a thing for Miss Felicity, so I was intrigued to meet her, even though the look of the shop left me cold.

The exterior brick had been painted black, with a lot of wrought iron scroll work around the lavender and gold striped window awnings and on the stair railings. The window display consisted of faceless mannequins in lavender wigs dressed in the kind of frilly and frou-frou-frumpy outfits that old ladies wear to tea or Sunday brunch. Faded plastic flowers peeked out from boxes perched below the display window.

I wouldn't be caught dead in a place like this.

To be fair, it used to be called 'The Merry Widow', and sold women's golf and tennis togs in pastel colors. In spite of the new look and fresh paint, my eyes seemed to slide right past it. Same old, same old.

I stepped up the short flight of steps and opened the door. Overhead a muted bell sounded in the back somewhere. The place was tiny—hardly as big as my old apartment living room. There was a lot more wrought iron here, spray-painted gold for a rich look. Instead of the expected green linoleum, the carpet was dark purple and cushy beneath my feet. Padded satin hangers held more silky old lady dresses like those in the window and some surprisingly sexy-looking lingerie.

The woman who bustled out from behind the purple drape looked familiar, but I couldn't place where I'd seen her before.

Felicity Caprice was a six-foot tall, round, voluptuous woman with black hair that she wore in a sort of loose bun on top of her head with several carefully cultivated stray curls trailing around her face. Attractive, in a high-maintenance sort of way. Fake eyelashes. Fake nails painted the same dark color as the carpet. Wearing four-inch spike heels, she towered more than a foot taller than me. Physically, more than a little intimidating. And similar to Mayor Brunson, she had an odd, murky-looking aura about her, although hers had a distinct maroon hue with a thread-thin crimson lifeline.

Definitely not the kind of woman I pictured with Mel. Mel was more of a gaunt, thrice-divorced, smoky-voiced blonde kind of a guy. I wondered what he saw in her.

Her dark eyes shone when she saw me, and for a brief moment, I felt like a rabbit facing a fox, but to give her credit, she acted thrilled to see me. She glanced down at my wrinkled culottes and practical work shoes, but didn't react.

"Welcome, welcome. I'm Felicity, how may I fulfill your dreams today?"

Oh great. I wished I'd brought Mimsy with me. She would have known how to handle this woman. But after she died the first time, Mimsy just wasn't the same. And after she died the second time, well, she wasn't going anywhere ever again.

"Um, Mel Moody sent me. I need a new uniform."

Her expression faltered. "Oh. Well dear, just bring it in and I'll have it stitched back together in no time."

"Um, well, there's no point. I tore it. It's ruined."

She frowned. "A whole new outfit? That won't come cheap, Miss..." Her eyes widened as she caught sight of my nametag, and her expression changed completely. "Oh good heavens, I can't believe it. Mattie Blackman, right here in my shop!" She laughed and pointed to a pale lavender banner draped across the back the store. "This is so perfect! It's fate that brought you to me, dear."

SPIRIT FESTIVAL HEADQUARTERS!
BE THE 'BELLE' OF THE BALL!
GET YOUR GOWN FOR THE GALA RIGHT HERE!

She clapped her hands. "Luçien, come out here!"

"Oh wait, no. I, I--." I froze, unable to speak, as the most starkly beautiful man I'd ever seen stepped out from behind the purple drape. I thought he was a model. Narrow build, with close-cropped hair which showed off his angular facial structure. Against his warm café-au-lait skin, pale blue eyes with long black lashes appraised me coolly. Built like a jockey, wiry and shorter even than me, but perfectly proportioned, in a dreamy sort of way. A cat-like smile played at the upturned corners of his full mouth.

He wore a black silk shirt with the sleeves rolled up to this elbows, and some sort of black filmy fabric that fitted him like a second skin. Pointy shoes. Italian— I'd bet my bra on it.

I snapped my jaw shut as he came toward me. He took my hand and held it to his lips as if it were the most natural thing in the world; his eyes never leaving mine. Pure animal magnetism.

He kissed the palm of my hand, inhaling my scent as if he were trying to memorize it. A little over-the-top, but my ego was loving it.

"Luçien, darling, this is Mattie Blackman. We were just talking about her the other day, and here she is in the flesh. Isn't that marvelous?"

"Mattie Blackman. This *is* a pleasure. Delicious to meet you." His lips burned like warm coals against my fingers.

I swallowed hard and pulled my hand back, albeit reluctantly. Luçien's eyes never left my face. I felt clumsy and out of my depth.

Felicity hovered closer. "Luçien is my nephew.

He's a fashion designer; come all the way from Italy just to spend the summer with me, isn't that sweet?"

"Lovely to meet you," I squeaked out. The three of us in that tiny shop had me feeling claustrophobic, like there wasn't enough air in the room.

"Mattie here is the Guest of Honor of the Spirit Festival. And *we're* going to design her gown for the ball!"

I broke away from Luçien's captivating stare turned to Felicity. "No, ah, I'm not here for a dress. Just the uniform, please."

Her face fell. "Oh. You mean you *already* have a Gala gown?"

I hesitated. Other than lying about it to Sheriff Reynolds, I hadn't given the ball much thought, and at this point in my post-burned-up-apartment life, I didn't have much of a wardrobe—much less a formal gown for the gala. I was sure that if I said no, that she'd try to sell me one of hers, and based on what I'd seen so far, her inventory was far too fussy and frumpy for my taste.

"Now, now, Auntie; first things first." Luçien came to my rescue. "If the Hand of Fate needs a new costume for work, you simply must make time for it. A rush job. How soon do you need it?" He stroked my hair. An odd, yet strangely intimate gesture.

A flood of images flashed through my mind, none of which were appropriate. Part of me lusted after him to do it again, but another, more distant part of me wondered what the hell he *was*. His lifeline, or what I could see of it, was a muddy brownish grey. Not human, although I had to admit I hadn't felt this attracted to a man since I'd met Rhys. And whatever he was, Luçien Bold was no *djenie*.

I forced my attention back to Felicity. "My next shift is Thursday night. Could I get it by then?" I hoped I'd brought enough cash to pay for it.

She thought for a moment before relenting. She gave me a beatific smile. "But of course, dear— on one condition. You simply *must* allow me to dress you for the ball as well." She waved her hands at me. "Everything—from panties to pinafore! You leave it all to me, dear."

Oh geeze. I hadn't really given any thought to what my participation in the Spirit Festival entailed. I'd lived here all my life but never attended a single one—it was just something for the tourists. I knew the opening ceremonies and gala would be held on the grounds of the amusement park, and that there was the parade that ran down Third Street during the middle of the week. The chamber of commerce already had posters up all over town, and local press always gave it a big write-up.

Now the big event was looming, I realized the cost of new duds would probably vaporize whatever money I had set aside for a deposit on an apartment, and then some. It was too late for me to back out—I'd given my word, and the posters already had my name on them. It was part of the whole Hand of Fate package I'd signed up for.

I took a second look at the shop's inventory. If I had to buy a dress, this would be the last place I'd look for one. Way too pricey and Felicity was the person who'd created those tacky flimsy costumes for Mel. I could only imagine what kind of ruffled horror she had in mind for me. "Well, I--."

Luçien gave me a slow grin. "I can promise you'll be more than satisfied with the results."

"And don't worry about the cost, dear. Think of it as a gift from me to you."

The weight their expectant faces got to me. How could I say no? It wouldn't kill me to support a local business.

"Okay, but I don't want anything too fancy. No ruffles."

"Of course, dear."

Two hours and a couple of pin jabs later, Felicity had taken my measurements and pinned several different swathes of brightly colored silk around me. I kept telling her I wanted something classic, but she kept talking about pick-ups, gussets, and ruching.

"And don't worry about the color, dear. Trust me; you'll be the belle of the ball. I know exactly what I'm doing. Just remember to tell everybody where you got your dress, eh? You can pick up your new uniform on Thursday."

I took a deep breath and told myself that this was the perfect solution—a win-win for everyone. Everything would work out just fine. "Thank you. That would be great."

CHAPTER 6

HE LEANED INTO me; his hypnotic blue eyes drained my will to resist as they stole the strength from my limbs. Naked and aroused, Luçien Bold lay on top of me, kissing me, easing me out of my shirt with deliberate slowness. His kisses burned my lips, my skin, everywhere he touched me. Part of me wanted him to hurry up, while somewhere in the back of my head some other part of me was thinking that this might not be a good idea. Like maybe I'd feel guilty in the morning, but not caring because I couldn't quite remember why.

I tried to push him away, but couldn't seem to move my arms.

My body thrummed to his touch and I noticed my bra gone too. I gasped the feel of his bare chest against mine. He reached for the zipper of my jeans—

Thwhack! "Again, Missy."

Cripes! I was back in Master Foo's studio. My

face burned with embarrassment. Not only because I had been dreaming of Luçien, but it felt like I'd been cheating on Rhys, and worst of all, the disgusted frown on Master Foo's normally placid face had me thinking that perhaps he had an idea what I'd been dreaming about.

This wasn't the first time I'd had this dream. And even after Master Foo's rude awakening, it still didn't feel like a dream. My skin still tingled and throbbed where Luçien had touched me. After such an abrupt awakening, I sure wasn't in the mood for meditation anymore.

Master Foo tapped me on the chest with this bamboo stick. "Physical practice is only a small part of Qhua Bei. Tell me, why are you here?"

I glanced around the studio and realized that Henri had already left. "I'm sorry, Master. I haven't been sleeping well. How long was I out?"

"The practice of meditation is *not* sleeping, but mindful awareness. It is the practice of attention and concentration. A discipline which, once mastered, will foster greater focus, mental acuity and a sense of physical and mental wellness. You seem to prefer dreaming to mindful awareness. So I ask again, Mattie Blackman—why are you here?"

"Ah, well, I need to learn self defense. Rhys thought--."

He poked me in the chest again. Harder, this

time. "No Missy. Why. Are. You. Here? Why do you come to me this week? Every week? I am a teacher. *What do you want to learn?*"

Million-dollar question and I didn't have an answer. This was not the first time he'd asked me this, but I got the feeling that it was probably the last. He was giving me a way out, if I wanted it. And last week, I would have been glad to quit, but now, for some reason I didn't want to. And I suspect he would accept nothing but bare honesty from me.

"I don't know, exactly—wait, no," I didn't want him to poke me again. "I mean you're going to think this is crazy, but I think I'm supposed to be here, only I just don't know why. But I think I'll know it when I learn it." I couldn't meet his eyes.

His expression didn't change, but he left the room, and when he came back, he handed me a palm-sized ten-minute hourglass and told me I could come back to study with him when I could close my eyes for ten minutes without falling asleep. Sheesh.

Lou Scali wouldn't tell me why Mayor Brunson had paid him to follow his cousin, Wiley Willy, so on Wednesday, I called his office. After putting me on hold for a couple minutes, his secretary, Jenna, told me he couldn't be disturbed at the moment, but to stop by the Mayor's office after I got off work.

Since we both work at the Picston City Hall, this was easy to do. At the end of my shift, I parked my three-wheeled patrol scooter in the lot and took the elevator up to the fourth floor. I'd been to the Mayor's office only once before, to get my picture taken with him for a commendation I'd received. The Mayor's suite consisted of a reception area, with a half-dozen cubicles for staff, and then a set of double doors leading to the Mayor's inner sanctum. Today, the doors were wide open. Looked like everyone had already left for the day. Brunson looked up at me as soon as I walked in.

"Hey, Mattie, good to see you." He gestured to a chair opposite a cherry wood desk as large as my bed. He looked tired, but his handshake was firm.

"Thanks, I just had a quick question--."

"I didn't get a chance to thank you for breaking the news to my aunt." His lips trembled and his expression turned to anguish. Clearly, the stress of Willy and Marjorie's deaths had hit him hard.

He wiped his mouth and tried again. "She was like a mother to me. Practically raised me. I know I should have been the one to tell her, but I just couldn't."

"I understand."

The role of Mayor was bigger to Jim Brunson than his own identity. He'd given up his personal life to serve his community, and he put his responsibility to the people of his community above his personal life. Jim Brunson had no wife or children. His constituents, both human and the paranormal, meant everything to him. He'd been outed as a paranormal during the election, but had managed to eke out a win anyway. By all accounts, he was generally thought of as a good Mayor, and the first to take a softer stance on the topic of the rights of Alternate Individuals. While the paranormal community gave him their admiration and support behind the scenes, he had no illusions that the priorities and sensibilities of his human constituents had to come first.

"I'm sorry about Willy." The image of Wiley Willy's jerkified corpse came back to me. "Hard to believe he'd been walking around just a few hours earlier. It doesn't make sense. Why did you hire Lou to follow him in the first place?"

If anything, Brunson just looked sadder. "You've got to understand. He wasn't just my cousin. He was—we were as close as bothers. He was younger than me, and always the wild one. He was still in junior high when I graduated and went on to RIT on a scholarship. I didn't have as much time for him, and I know he resented it. He starting hanging out with a rough group. Got into trouble. He dropped out of school—he never did finish. By the time Aunt Marjorie asked me to do something, he was in pretty deep with a bad crowd."

Brunson took a deep breath and got up to stand

in front of the big picture window, which looked out downtown Picston. "After more than a few false starts, he got into music. He'd always played bass guitar. Then he started singing. He joined a couple of bands, and then he started up his own. The music seems to turn him around.

Brunson turned back to me, his hands in his pockets. "He was really good, you know. Had a couple of agents snooping around, trying to get him to move to New York, but he wouldn't. I think he didn't want to leave Marjorie and maybe, to a lesser extent, me." He gave a rueful grin. "I like to think I was part of that decision, too. Because after he started up Wiley Willy and the Rogues, he came into his own, and we were tight again."

"So why did you hire Lou?"

"There was something wrong. He started looking bad. He wasn't eating and I don't think he was sleeping very well. I recognized the signs from before, and was worried. I thought--." His mouth trembled and he struggled for composure.

"Take your time."

"I thought he was in trouble again. One of the band members quit and they hired a guy from Buffalo. He had a big following and Willy thought it would help the band, but I thought he was a bad influence. I was afraid Willy was going to, ah, end up in trouble again. That's why I had Lou follow him. I wanted to know what was going on."

"And did he find out anything?"

Brunson shook his head. "It was too soon to tell. But I think Marjorie knew. Did she tell you?" His eyes filled with tears and he turned back to the window.

My heart went out to him. "She didn't say anything about that, but she knew why I was there. Before she, um, passed, she said some things that I didn't understand. I thought you might know what she was talking about."

His expression became guarded. "What did she say?"

"She said to trust the vampires. Does that make any sense?"

He stiffened. "You must understand. I loved Aunt Marjorie, but she had a good many friends in the vampire community. She was absolutely blind to their utter lack of any redeeming qualities. They're vindictive, petty, and jealous of--." He stopped himself. "Let me just say that their whisper campaign against me very nearly lost me the election. You cannot give any credence to anything she said about vampires. They cannot be trusted."

Sheesh. Hard to believe his opinion and Marjorie's were so far apart. "She mentioned a woman named Neldene."

For the merest second, he gaped at me like a fish caught on a line, but immediately recovered. "Never heard of her. Probably one of Aunt Marjorie's cronies."

As Luke would say, I felt a disturbance in the force. Mayor Jim Brunson had just lied to me. "Really? She said something about Neldene designing the dresses for the Festival."

"Nope. Sorry, doesn't ring a bell."

Another lie.

"Hey," he brightened. "Are you ready for next week? Did Enzo get hold of you?"

Enzo Obote is Mayor Brunson's former campaign manager, and chairman of this year's Spirit Festival. The men have been best friends since college and are as different as, well, black and white. Brunson is a quiet and reserved, while Enzo electrifies a room just by walking into it. He's a high energy guy, president of the Picston Chamber of Commerce, and runs his own design firm, Mojo Boogie. Of the two of them, Enzo is by far the more likely to be a political animal, but he prefers to work behind the scenes, and he's good at it. He managed to get Brunson elected as New York's first paranormal Mayor, in spite of being outed as such in the middle of the campaign.

"Pretty much." I counted off my responsibilities on my fingers. "Opening ceremonies Monday evening at the amusement park. I help you cut the ribbon and pose for pictures. Wednesday is the parade—I guess we're supposed to be at the assembly point in the Lakeshore Bank parking lot at 11:30am."

The City of Picston wanted me to wear my

uniform for both the ribbon-cutting ceremony and the parade. Such is small-town politics. It was Shore Haven's Festival, but Picston's contributions wouldn't be overlooked. Lucky me, I wouldn't even have to take the day off. All I had to do was smile and wave to the crowd as we drove by in a posh Cadillac convertible. Not a bad gig.

I shrugged. "And then the Gala on Saturday night..." I forced a smile. "All set."

The moment stretched between us. "You got a dress yet?"

"Why does everybody keep asking me that?" Enzo had been particularly insistent.

"I take that as a no. Get your ass in gear, girl. You've got this whole town in the palm of your hand during Festival week. If you don't look good, we don't look good. Lot of outsiders coming in here to see just what kind of person the new Hand of Fate is going to be. Madame Coumlie was strong. She kept the riff-raff in line, and everybody had a good time. But you're an unknown. Some paranormal folks will be looking at Shore Haven as some kind of place to set up their own fiefdoms. You're the one who will set the tone for the whole community. If you're too weak, they'll think they can move in and take over; too strong and they'll think we'll be ripe for change. You've got to be like, 'Welcome, fans. Have fun, spend your money, and mind your manners, 'cause we don't accept anything less.' You've got to look the part."

Enzo had said as much. The Picston badge on my uniform indicated I was an authority figure, and lend credibility to the Hand of Fate. Enzo had also lectured me on the importance of the gala. The gown had to be something special.

The Mayor reached into his desk drawer and pulled out a business card. "This is a card for Felicity Caprice, the chairwoman for the Gala. She runs a dress shop in Shore Haven. She's providing uniforms and costumes for all the staff—even the band. We want everyone to look good."

"We already met. She offered to make me a gown for the Gala."

"Excellent! You're in good hands then."

It wasn't until I was out in the parking lot that I realized that hadn't told me anything at all about what kind of trouble he thought Wiley Willy was in.

CHAPTER 7

LUÇIEN PULLED DOWN the zipper of my jeans with agonizing slowness. My thighs felt as if they were on fire. His warm full lips on my bare belly had me arching my back in spite of myself. I had no control over my extremities. I tried to twist away...

He began tapping my naked chest with his chin. What an odd movement--.

Blix, my little *djemon* was jumping up and down on my chest, highly agitated. His glowing yellow eyes wide with angst. Irritated, I started to shove him off me, but stopped when I smelled smoke. The sounds of approaching fire engines spurred me to action.

I threw off the covers and reached for my robe, all the while yelling for Henri. Through the voile curtains, I could see flames flickering on the roof of a rental house a few doors down the street. It was another of those big 'painted lady' Victorian homes which line Empress Street. The hundred-year-old homes in Shore

Haven stand very close together and are built of wood—most with outmoded electrical systems. A fire at one house could very well threaten the whole town.

Henri met me at the bottom of the stairs and we ran outside to see if we could help. Three fire trucks were already on the scene, and had their hoses turned on the flames. The water kept the flames from spreading, but the house itself looked like a total loss.

As Henri and I lingered on the sidewalk with our neighbors, I heard my name mentioned from somewhere behind me.

"Mattie, hey Mattie."

It was Juno Rockover, the new bass player for Wiley Willy and the Rogues. Or, I guess, just the Rogues, now. He was a big name in the Buffalo music scene. I'd heard that he'd joined up with Wiley Willy for the Spirit Festival gig. Before he moved to Buffalo, he'd lived in Shore Haven, and we'd gone to the same elementary school and Junior High. Juno was a couple years older than me, so I'd never really hung out with him, but guess I knew him well enough by sight.

Well enough to know he wasn't human anymore. No lifeline. There was something wrong with him. All of them. Their eyes were too black and shiny—their skin almost glowed with an unhealthy shade of pale.

When he grabbed my arm, he smelled of soot and smoke and blood.

Alarmed, I tried to pull away, but he gripped

me like a drowning man reaching for a life preserver. "I need your help."

Henri, standing next to me, let out a shout. "Oh man, you're Juno Rockover! I listen to your music all the time! It's a thrill to meet you!" He patted his ever-present ear-buds. "I'm listening to you right now! Huge fan, man."

Juno let go of my arm and numbly shook Henri's outstretched hand. "Oh yeah? That's great." He turned his gaze to mine. "Come on, Mattie, we don't have much time. The fire department won't let us back into the house. Dawn will be here in a few hours and we need a safe place where we can crash."

Instinctively, I stepped back, trying to figure out what I was seeing. Part of me wanted to run away, but my Scooby senses were tingling, and I just *had* to figure out what had happened to him.

He shook his head. "No wait, that's not right. I've got to say the words." His gaze held mine. "Um, the band and I formally request sanctuary with the Hand of Fate."

The little door in my mind where Morta lives blew wide open and I gaped at the three desperate undead men standing before me. They belonged to me. Or, Morta, at any rate. They were part of her realm, and had formally asked for my protection. I nodded, not even certain what I was saying yes to.

Dimly, I felt Henri pounding me on the back, his enthusiasm clear. "Hell yes! We've got plenty of room!

The basement is perfect for you guys. You can sleep all day without being disturbed."

It hit me then. Sometime in the last twenty years, Juno Rockover had become a vampire.

Relief flooded the three men's faces. "Thanks, man," Juno said. "I can't tell you how much that means to us."

"This is so great!" Henri grabbed me in a big bear hug. "Can you believe it, Mattie? Juno Rockover and the band are going to be our new roommates!"

Greaaat.

CHAPTER 8

"We'd just come back from playing a club in Rochester," Juno told me, as we carried the band's equipment down to the basement of Madame Coumlie's house. "Good thing, too, or our equipment would've gone up in smoke. We all tried to get in there to look for Eddie, but we couldn't find him."

Eddie Reale was the band's sax player.

"Why wasn't he with you?" I asked. I was still feeling uncomfortable about sharing a house with a bunch of vampires, but Juno assured me that biting the Hand of Fate was taboo for vamps, and Henri's inhuman blood didn't appeal to them. And Henri was so very delighted to have them stay with us.

"He hadn't been feeling well lately," answered Ray Mackie, the drummer. Ray had been hired to take the place of Kid Harsh, the guy Lou told me about who'd ended up as road kill a few weeks back. "Said he was really wiped out. We could play without him, so we left for the gig."

"We were lucky," Mike Weyland ran his hand through his dirty blonde hair and shook his head. "I hope Eddie was too. I hope he got out."

"This is no coincidence, Mattie," Juno said. In the harsh light of the basement, he had that ageless look that a lot of rock and rollers get. Not young, but not exactly old either. Far older than Wiley Willy looked, that's for sure. I guess being a vampire in a rock band is a hard life. "Someone is targeting the band. First Kid Harsh, then Buddy, then William. Speaking for all of us, we're spooked."

"Who is Buddy?" asked Henri. He was still a bit starry-eyed and hung on every word and gesture Juno made.

"Buddy Ramone was our keyboardist," Mike said. "One of the original band members. He disappeared a week after we moved into the house. He and Willy argued about the play list Enzo had given us." He gave a rueful smile. "Actually, none of were real happy with it. Buddy got real hot and took off. He never came back—and I mean *never*. Nobody could find him. We filed a police report, but he never showed up."

"That's when I came in," Juno interjected. "William and I go way back—all the way to junior high. He didn't want to back out of the Festival at the last minute, and it's the band's biggest paycheck of the year." He shrugged. "He called in a favor."

"Must've been some favor," Ray said, as he twirled a drumstick between his fingers. "Given the play list."

Juno grinned. "Hey I dig that music!"

Ray and Mike both groaned.

"What's wrong with the music?" I asked.

"We're pretty much a rock band," explained Ray. "We like the hard stuff, mixed with a bit of blues—you know, party music, that kind of thing. But this--."

"Enzo wanted the music for the Spirit Ball this year to compliment the theme of the Festival" Juno explained. "Karma. You know, the whole what goes around, comes around thing. I guess musically, Enzo is stuck in the '70's."

"So?"

"So disco. New age funk." Ray stared tapping out an intro beat on the drums and Ray plugged his guitar into the amp.

"And boogie," added Juno, his fingers skipped across his keyboard briefly, and then he hit the chords for an intro. A few bars later, the guys started jamming, and soon were belting out a chorus of Age *of Aquarius*. Sheesh. They were in their own little world. Henri was transfixed—like they were superheroes or something.

I felt like I'd just been dismissed; like I wasn't even the room. I stared at them. I'd heard vampires didn't have the same attachments as humans, but *hello, your house just burned up...?* I tried to say something, but the music was too loud, and Juno wouldn't look at me. Mike just grinned and shook his head. Never missed a note.

I can take a hint. I climbed the stairs to my room, and flopped down onto the bed. Even from two floors above the basement, the walls of my bedroom throbbed with every note. No chance of getting any sleep with that racket going on. I closed my eyes to collect my thoughts.

To be honest, the whole night felt surreal. Hard to believe I'd just spent an hour in the basement talking about music with a bunch of vampires. Or that they'd asked *me* for protection. Of course Henri didn't need to invite them to move in with us, but it was his house, so I had no place to say he couldn't. But knowing how little experience Henri had being, well, alive, I should probably talk to him about it.

Juno was right. With Buddy Ramone, Kid Harsh, and Wiley Willy all dead or missing, that was too much of a coincidence. Someone was targeting the band. Who would do such a thing? And why? What could the motivation be?

Money? That would be the obvious choice. Juno said it himself—the Festival was the band's biggest paycheck of the year. He didn't say how much, but easy enough to find out. Weird that Ray, Mike and Juno were all vampires. I wondered if Wiley Willy had been a vampire. I tried to remember if I'd ever seen him play in the daytime. I was pretty sure I had. I didn't know about Buddy Ramone or Kid Harsh, though. Lou would probably know.

Or Rhys.

Dang it all, where the hell was he? I checked my cell phone for messages. Still no word from Rhys. It felt like forever since I'd heard from him. Nearly three weeks—even then, it had just been a text saying he'd be in touch soon. I wondered if he'd changed his mind about me. Maybe he'd decided not to come back from Scotland after all. The guy had been around for a couple thousand years. Probably had a lot of girlfriends. I closed my eyes, trying to do the math in my head. Figure one a year, at least for two thousand years, sheesh. He probably couldn't remember them all. Hell, I was already having kind of a hard time remembering his face—a depressing thought.

And suddenly, Luçien was there was and my thoughts turned a completely different direction.

The alarm jolted me out of another sex dream with Luçien. More of a nightmare, really. I was helpless. My lips were sealed and couldn't move my arms or legs. My clothes were gone and everywhere his lips touched me, I burned for more, even as I didn't want him to do those things that only Rhys had permission to do. I woke up feeling guilty, unsatisfied, and cranky. *Damn it Rhys, where are you?*

All was quiet in the basement, so I guess Juno and the guys were down for the day. I showered and dressed for work, but for once Henri wasn't there to have breakfast with me. Understandable, I guess. Last night had been disruptive for both of us. Still, I felt as if I should talk to him about taking in vampires as boarders.

At the end of my shift, when I went out to my car in the parking lot, Lou was waiting for me, leaning up against the hood of Trusty Rusty, looking about as relaxed as I've ever seen him.

"Talked to your lawyer yet?" he asked, before I could say anything.

"Fontaigne?" My heart skipped a beat. "No, why? What happened?"

He grinned. "The investigation into Wiley Willy's murder has been dropped."

I looked around the parking lot to make sure no one was close enough to hear. "Tell me!"

"My source in the coroner's office tells me the body had been drained of fluids, but the coroner could not determine the exact manner of death. They found a set of fang marks on the body."

Ah, so maybe Willy *was* a vampire. I frowned. That couldn't be right. Brunson hated vampires. I was so tired I couldn't think straight. "We didn't see any vampire bites on the body."

"Not *vampire* bites, no. The post mortem revealed a nearly invisible bite on the inner thigh, but it wasn't vampire. Coroner says he thinks it's a bug bite or some type of snake."

"Snakebite?" That didn't sound right. I thought about my previous conversation with Mayor Brunson. What would he be so worried about that he'd hire Lou to follow him? If Wiley Willy wasn't a vampire, maybe it was drugs. "Could it have been a needle marks?"

"I asked, but the dude was definitely envenomated. The toxins attacked the major organs of his body and liquefied them. Whatever bit him sucked out all his blood and the liquefied interior organs as well. The bite wasn't what killed him—he was still alive while he was being sucked dry. Eventually his heart stopped."

"That's disgusting."

"Yeah."

Something bothered me about this whole thing. My old Scooby senses were kicking at me like crazy. "Mayor Brunson and Madame Marjorie both seemed to think he was involved with something dangerous. Now you're telling me he died of a snake bite. Don't you think that's a bit odd?" I tried to think how Wiley Willy might have encountered a poisonous snake in one of those cabins. And wait, snakes ate their prey whole. They didn't suck them dry like a milkshake. "What kind of snake?"

Lou shrugged. "They're still working on that. Something exotic, I guess. They've sent samples to the San Diego Zoo for analysis." He frowned. "Hey, what's the deal? I thought you'd be glad to hear you're off the hook for his murder."

"Oh I am, but something doesn't feel right. What about Marjorie?" My thoughts felt muzzy from lack of sleep.

Lou shook his head sadly. "She was dying of cancer, probably would have been dead in a week anyway. Against doctor's advice, she'd stopped her chemotherapy six months earlier—decided to go with a holistic approach. Coroner figures the shock of her son's death finished her off."

I remembered Marjorie telling me she'd known that her son was going to die. Maybe that was when she decided she didn't want to live anymore, either. So sad. Had she known he'd die of a *snake bite*? "When you said he was bitten, I was pretty sure I was a vampire."

"Vampires only drink blood, Mattie. This thing took everything."

He was right. Definitely not vampire. "So hey, both Marjorie and Brunson were worried about him. Why did Brunson hire you, anyway? Was it drugs? Or something else?"

"I told you to ask Brunson."

"I did. He was pretty vague about it. Something

about Willy hanging out with the wrong crowd. Look, he's dead, and I think the band is being targeted." I told him about the fire down the street and giving sanctuary to what remained of the band. "That's three of the band members either missing or dead. That's too big of a coincidence to ignore. Come on, Lou, help me out here."

He raised his eyebrows. "No many would open their home to a vampire, much less a whole pack."

"I didn't, exactly. It was Henri's idea. And they did promise not to bite."

"Riight."

"Hey, it's not like I'm happy having them there, but they asked for my protection. I guess staying with Henri and me is about as safe as anywhere. Come on; tell me why Brunson hired you."

Lou seemed to come to a decision. "Okay, here it is. I got the same sort of runaround from Brunson when he hired me to follow his cousin. Nothing specific. But then the coroner turned up something in the autopsy that explained a lot of things, including maybe why Brunson was trying to keep an eye on Willy and why it had to be kept quiet. I doubt even the press will hear about this." He tapped his notebook. "Seems that Wiley Willy was a dhampir."

I was so tired, I thought I hadn't heard him right. "A *what*?"

"*Dhampir*. A daywalker. Half human, half vampire."

I shook my head. "Vampires are dead. They can't reproduce."

Lou gave me a disgusted look. "If you're gonna be the Hand of Fate in this town, Mattie, you're gonna have to educate yourself. Male vamps have viable sperm for weeks after they're first risen. It's not as unusual as you'd think. I imagine Jim Brunson is shittin' bricks right now. The folks in this town will forgive him for being a paranormal, but if it gets out that he's got vampires in his family tree, he'll never hold public office again."

Dhampirs. Never heard of them. But it made sense, sort of. "Brunson must be a dhampir, too. Makes perfect sense, actually." Juno and Willy had been friends a long time, maybe even since before Juno was made a vampire. Of course Brunson wouldn't want to see his cousin involved with vamps, right? My head began to pound. If only I could think straight. So many questions—I had to get some sleep.

"And there's more." He flipped the page on his notepad. "You ready for this? This morning the arson investigator found the remains of a charred body in the ashes of that house fire down the street from you. The identification is pending, but based on dog tags they found around his neck, they're pretty sure it will check out." Lou glanced at his notes. "Guy by the name of Eddie Reale. You know him?"

My legs began to tremble and I sat on the curb,

trying to sort out my thoughts. "Yeah. Well, I know the name. He played saxophone for the Rogues."

"The fire was caused by a faulty wire, but the word I got was that Eddie was dead before the fire broke out. The coroner said there was no evidence of smoke particulants in his sinuses or nasal cavity. He also said Eddie's lungs and internal organs were missing, just like Willy Parry's."

I gave him a hard stare. "That's four, Lou. Four members of the band are dead. We've got to find out who's doing this and stop him."

CHAPTER 9

I HAD NO idea how to find out who had a reason to kill off Wiley Willy and the Rogues, but Lou was on it, and I trusted his instincts. Besides, between working two jobs and the upcoming Spirit Festival, I was so busy, I couldn't do much anyway. On Thursday, I went into Les Belles Jolie to pick up my new uniform for work and had my first fitting for the gown I would be wearing to the Spirit Ball. Henri went with me, in part because I wanted his opinion on the dress, and in part because I wanted him as backup in case that Luçien Bold guy made a pass at me.

Yeah, I knew it was silly to think he was really *in* my dreams, but those titillating dream trysts had rapidly evolved into thigh-clenching nightmares. I couldn't resist him—not even a little, and every time I fell asleep, he was there—getting closer to rape each time. Not only that, but he seemed to be enjoying my panic. And besides, I still hadn't figured out what

Luçien Bold *was*, and I had a very bad feeling that if he actually raped me in my dream, that something very bad would happen.

"Hello, dearie," Felicity crushed Henri and me to her ample bazongas. She whisked a familiar-looking shred of black fabric pinned to a padded lavender hangar and laid it out on the glass countertop. "Your new uniform is all ready, just as promised." I felt the blood drain from my face as she presented me with the bill. I handed over two weeks' worth of tips without a word. "And I've thrown in three pair of my signature panties with my compliments. As I was taking your measurements last time, I couldn't help but notice the, shall we say, pedestrian quality of your unmentionables? A pretty thing like you should be wearing something far more feminine next to your skin. I guarantee my silk lingerie will give you a whole new outlook."

She led us into the back of the store to her workroom, a surprisingly spacious room with a large antique pine worktable, a half-dozen dressmaker's dummies, and hundreds of bolts of fabric stacked against the sandblasted brick walls. In the back corner, a circular iron stairway led upstairs, presumably to Felicity's living quarters. Chrystal chandeliers illuminated the room with a warm glow, and softened the workman-like effect of the clutter of pins and scissors, and accouterments of her profession.

There was no sign of Luçien, for which I was hugely relieved. Henri settled himself onto a pouf near the coffee maker, closed his eyes, and plugged in his ear buds. I could tell he was meditating—something I should have been practicing, but frankly, I didn't want to risk falling asleep and meeting up with Luçien.

Felicity pulled a curtain across the fitting area and had me strip to my undies and step up to a low platform for the fitting. The fabric was the same sort of filmy see-through stuff as my uniform, except this was an unflattering beige color. Ugh.

"I was hoping for something with a little color," I said with as much tact as I could muster.

Felicity giggled through a mouthful of pins and quickly transferred them to a pincushion on her wrist. "No dear, this is the muslin pattern fabric." She crossed the room and picked up a bolt of silvery turquoise-blue fabric, which rippled and flowed around her as she brought it over for me to inspect. "Theraphos silk—the finest and rarest silk in the world. It's tougher and more resilient than regular silk, and completely waterproof. Lighter than down, stronger than steel. I've been saving it for something special, and here you are."

The fabric was incredibly lightweight, and felt comfortably warm against my skin. "It's beautiful." And it was.

I must've been there for over an hour before she finished pinning and primping the fabric around me. I couldn't really tell much, other than the neckline plunged far deeper than I was comfortable with, and the skirt volume was enormous. I could have used it for a parachute.

"Oh don't worry about that dearie. You've a lovely figure, and besides, we have to make room for all the ruffles—no no, don't fret. I promise you'll be stunned with the results."

Ruffles. It *had* to be ruffles. "You know, I'm not really a ruffles kind of girl--."

She gave me a hard look. "Now now. You must trust me. When you make your entrance at the Spirit Ball, all eyes will be on you. And isn't that what we want? What *you* want? This is, after all, *your* coming out to the whole community, is it not? After the Spirit Ball, the whole world will know about Shore Haven's new Hand of Fate. Believe me; the old Hand of Fate never looked this good."

The steel in her voice shut down my protest. I hadn't really thought about it like that. This dress was not about me or what I wanted. It was about the paranormal community in Shore Haven. Anyway, it was only for one night—just a few hours, tops. I did like the color and ruffles or no, it was too late to back out now. She'd probably had the ruffles in mind all along. Dang it, I hate it when I'm right.

As it was, I was too tired to argue. I stumbled home in a fog, clutching my new uniform with a mixture of contempt and victory. I had three hours before my shift started, and nothing would stand between me and a nap.

For once, Luçien didn't show. But it seemed like I'd hardly closed my eyes at all before the sun went down and the Juno Rockover and the guys started practicing in the basement. I lay there with my eyes closed, the walls of my bedroom vibrating with the base beat, while Blix snuggled up against my neck. I didn't sleep, but when got up to go to work, I felt better than I had in days. Maybe there was something to this mediation thing after all.

Thursday night and Friday passed in a blur. On Saturday I had to get up early for another fitting with Felicity. Henri had some time to kill before his session with Master Foo, so he came with me to Les Belles Jolie for my second fitting. Once again, there was no sign of Luçien.

"What do you think?" I stepped out from behind the screen. Felicity fussed with the ruffled neckline while I tried to push up the bell-shaped long sleeves. Even with the plunging vee-neck and back. I was swimming in a sea of fabric.

"Oh it's just lovely, dear. The color brings out

the ah, yellow of your eyes.

Sheesh. I'd forgotten to put in my contacts. What's more, I was so tired, I didn't care. I faced the mirror. It was a struggle to keep my expression neutral. Under normal circumstances, I wouldn't be caught dead in the thing. "What do you think, Henri? Come on, I want your opinion."

Henri barely glanced in my direction before looking away. His hands thrummed lightning-fast tattoo on this thighs. "Take off those ridiculous sleeves, rip out the ruffles and cut about four feet of fabric off the bottom. Throw in a pair of thigh-high strappy stilettos and we might be able to do something with it." He closed his eyes, lost in the music which even plugged into his ears is loud enough to hear from across the dressing room.

Felicity glared at Henri, her lips pursed in disapproval. "I hardly think--."

He was right. This thing looked more like a granny's nightgown on me than a ball gown. I held up my hands in appeasement. "Sorry, I shouldn't have asked." I turned before the mirror, the light fabric swirled around me like a silver-blue mist. "I do like the color; maybe it would look better without the sleeves. I think it will be too hot--."

"Now, now, dearie, trust me. This dress is not supposed to look like something you wore to your prom." She tugged on one of the sleeves, marking the hem at the end of my fingertips. "I've worked my fingers to the bone the last couple of months, creating the garments for most of Shore Haven's spirit community, including the staff. I know what they're wearing. This gown will outshine them all."

It began as it always did, with me lying on my back and Luçien crawling up my body. This time, I was naked, except for the wispy lingerie Felicity Caprice had given me. I tried to scream, but no sound came out. Luçien's lips on my bare skin had me responding to him, even though I didn't want it. This was definitely creepy now. It didn't matter how handsome he was, I didn't want him. I struggled to move, but that seemed to encourage him.

Something really, really bad was going to happen. I had to wake up. But I couldn't. I yelled at him to stop, but that just seemed to encourage him. He slipped his hand inside my panties.

I tried to concentrate on something else; anything—just to get my mind off of what he was doing to me. I remembered Master Foo's words about meditation. Meditation wasn't sleep. It was breathing. Feel your breath. Fill your lungs to beyond their fullest, and then a teeny bit more. Then release the air from the top of the lungs to the bottom, and a beat beyond the point where there was no more air left.

It was no use. 'Stop it. I want you to stop what

you're doing right now,' I said.

He rubbed his thumb against me, and to my horror, by body responded. 'It's my nature,' he told me, 'I'm a dreamstrider. It's what I do, from the day of my birth until the day I die. I know you want me."

His fingers were relentless. To my horror, an irresistible tension build within me. 'Stop that,' I said, but my voice sounded weak. 'Please,' I gasped.

He paused just short of the inevitable. 'Why should I?'

I blew the air from my lungs in a long steady exhale. 'I don't want you to.'

He laughed. 'They never do.' He lowered his head to my stomach and began to nuzzle his way lower.

With a sudden gasp, I was fully awake. I sat bolt upright on the bed, my pulse pounding.

That was no dream.

CHAPTER 10

THE REST OF the weekend passed in a haze—I was terrified to fall asleep. Graveyard shift at Dave's Killer Burgers on Saturday night was crazy—the place was packed with out-of-town visitors in for the festival; some human, some not even close. Juno Rockover and the band stopped by, and he brought a half-dozen other vampires with them. They didn't come to eat—they wanted to see me feed the piranhas. I was so tired; I almost fell asleep with my head on the edge of the tank.

Within hours of learning of Eddie's death in the fire, Juno had hired a fourth vampire to join the band in the basement. Juno knew the new sax player from Buffalo, and the band was practicing pretty much from dusk to dawn. While I admired Juno's commitment to fulfill Wiley Willie's contract, I wondered how sincere he was, or if he had a motive to getting rid of Wiley Willy and the band. One gig didn't seem a big enough motive to kill over, but maybe there was something in their childhood history—a grudge, maybe. Of course, with the band practicing all night, I was getting no real sleep at all—just a light doze. The only real benefit to that was that Luçien Bold stayed out of my dreams.

For the umpteenth time, I wished Rhys hadn't left. Not just because I missed him and thought that maybe Luçien wouldn't be able to invade my dreams so easily, but for other reasons, too. Rhys was smart, and probably knew a lot more about local vampire history than I did. Besides, he owned Mystic Properties, and knew all the places in town that would rent to paranormals, including vampires. He'd be able to find the band a safe place where they could practice, I was certain. I felt like I was stumbling around in the dark here.

After work on Monday, I drove out to Heavenly Shores Amusement Park for the ribbon-cutting ceremony, which marked the official opening of the week-long Spirit Festival. The park was already full of visitors, many of whom were in costumes, some even in native dress—everything from aliens to zombies. I wandered along the manicured paths I'd known so well from childhood, but had never visited during the festival. The place had been transformed.

Any other weekend during the summer, the shrill screams of kids and adults echoed through the manicured gardens as visitors enjoyed the thrills of the wooden roller coaster, the parachute drop, and even the carousel. Twenty minutes before the ribbon-cutting ceremony, the rides were temporarily halted.

I strolled through a tent village of colorful booths set along the wide path, of fortune-tellers, astrologers, weavers, artists, healers, chakra cleansers, oracles, reiki masters, numerologists, and cyberneticists, in an unending variety. Other areas were set aside as places for practitioner worship for both followers and the curious, as well as classes, music, and even an unnatural history museum housed in a big-top circus tent boasting a cryptid zoo.

Even the food was different. Instead of the smells of barbeque and kettle corn, the vibrant scent of exotic spices and curries filled the air. I knew most of the food would probably be vegetarian, gluten-free, dairy-free, and probably taste-free too, but it sure smelled good. My stomach rumbled. I wanted to get something to eat, but everything for sale looked either sticky or gooey or drippy or all three.

The Shore Haven Chamber of Commerce had made a request through the Mayor's office for me to wear my work uniform for the ribbon ceremony, so as to lend a bit of credibility to the whole Hand of Fate image.

Enzo told me that this was supposed to tie-in with the whole what-goes-around-comes-around theme of this year's festival. I didn't have the nerve to ask how a meter maid uniform improved the credibility of the spirit festival, but Enzo must've known what I was thinking.

"Think of it this way, Mattie. For the last seventy-five years, Shore Haven's paranormal community has been living in a shadow world—hiding in plain sight as it were. As much as Madame Coumlie was loved and respected by the people who knew her, she was minimized by her age and appearance by the prejudice of outsiders. Only her reputation as the Hand of Fate kept the underworld of Shore Haven safe from those who would seek to prey on them. And now here you come along, a marketer's dream—young, athletic, attractive, and an officer of the law. What's not to like?"

So no matter how good the food smelled, I had to be sure that whatever I got to eat, it wouldn't make a mess on my white shirt.

I settled on something called Devils & Angels. Bite-sized cubes of chocolate and angel-food cake, deep fried and dipped in a hard chocolate shell, served up with strawberry dipping sauce. They even gave me a plastic bib. After the first bite, I'm certain I experienced some sort of spiritual epiphany—I swore I would never eat cake again unless it was deep-fried and dipped in chocolate.

Mayor Brunson found me as I finished the last delectable bite. "Hey Mattie, I need another favor."

I gave him my best smile. Like almost getting arrested for Wiley Willy's murder wasn't enough. "Of course."

"The joint viewing for William and Marjorie will

be tomorrow night, and as per her wishes, Neldene is hosting it, so I won't be going."

So I guess Brunson *had* heard of her after all. "Why not?"

"Neldene is a vampire. She was Marjorie's best friend. They'll all be there. Enrique and his cronies just about cost me the election. I won't jeopardize my position by attending a vampire function. I won't give them the satisfaction. I would consider it a huge personal favor if you would go in my place. You're about the only person who *could* go to the viewing in my stead without it being seen as an insult."

To be perfectly honest, the idea of spending and evening in a funeral parlor with a bunch of vampires had about as much appeal as a root canal, but since the alternative was going home to a houseful of vampires playing loud music all night, I figured the peace and quiet would do me good. "Yeah, sure. No problem." Brunson promised to email me the specifics, as the ribbon-cutting ceremony was finished.

The ceremony itself was short, if not sweet. Everyone was given a rainbow ribbon sash with their title emblazoned in silver glitter. Mine said simply, 'Miss Fate'. Give me a break. Someone actually thought my first name was 'Hand of'?

I hated it.

Miss Fate. Sounded like mis-fate. Like a bad omen. I wondered if Madame Coumlie had ever worn a

'Miss Fate' ribbon. I couldn't imagine she would have. Not in a million years.

Mayor Brunson and I shared the honors, and the rainbow-colored ribbon was cut on the second try, after which I was pretty much out of the picture. In addition to Mayor Brunson, and Enzo Obote, there were a couple dozen other dignitaries, and of course, the queen of silken flounces herself, Felicity Caprice, chairwoman of the Spirit Ball. I figured out pretty quick it was a photo-op for the local business owners and sponsors, and ditched my misfortunate sash in the nearest trashcan.

Twenty minutes later, the photographers and news people left, and most of the other dignitaries began to drift off toward their air-conditioned vehicles. I saw Felicity make a bee-line for the park's ballroom. Probably working on the decorations. Suddenly the answer to half my problems became clear. I caught up with Enzo Obote, the Spirit Festival Chairman just as he was heading out to the parking lot.

"Hey Enzo, you got a minute?"

He beamed when he saw me, then frowned as he checked his watch. "A quick one. What's up?"

"It's about the band. With Willy gone, and the fire this week, the band has had to bring in some new members. They need a place to practice." I pointed in the direction of the park's Grand Ballroom, in the center of the park. "Is there any chance they could use the ballroom? Just until Saturday?"

Enzo briefly considered it. "It would have to be after the park closes."

I didn't know if Enzo knew that the band was all vamps, but it wasn't my place to say. "That's perfect for these guys."

"Fine. I'll make the arrangements." He was already pulling out his cell phone. "I'll let Charlie Crimmer know. He can let them in and lock after them. Anything else?"

Mattie Blackman for the score! I couldn't believe my luck. "No, that's great, thank you." I grinned. I couldn't wait to tell the Juno and the band. Everything was going to work out perfect.

"You all set for the parade Wednesday?"

"Yep. Can't wait." I showed him my parade wave. "See?"

He laughed. "See you then." And he was gone.

Henri showed up just then, and we decided to check out the big tent with the unnatural history museum.

Charlie Crimmer, one of the park's security guards, was on duty at the entrance to the big tent. "Hey there, Mattie," he growled with the husky voice of a lifelong smoker. "Enzo just gave me the word about the band. Don't you worry 'bout a thing. I'll make sure they get in alright. Be kinda nice to have some comp'ny here late at night."

Charlie is a psychopomp, and under my special protection. He escorts the souls of the dead through one of the portals to the underworld, which just so happens to sit beneath the funhouse at Heavenly Shores Amusement Park. He's also a demon master, like me, albeit an unwilling one. I accidently tore a hole in his soul when he came to me to banish his djemon, and the only way I could repair it, was to plug in a new one. Annie, a djemon who'd been torn from her master's soul, was dying when I brought her to Charlie. They'd healed each other. Yeah, in more ways than one, Charlie was one of mine.

"Thanks, Charlie."

"You and Henri go right on in. Yer money's no good here this week."

The unnatural history museum, was a bit of a letdown, but interesting nonetheless. The museum part was jars of specimens salvaged from old side shows and taxidermied creations like jackalopes, shrunken heads, and fish-tailed monkeymaids. Also collections of butterflies, insects, bird eggs, crystals, and a fascinating array of artifacts.

Henri and I must've caught the old curator's eye, because he came over and introduced himself. "Abe Leightner, at your service, Madame." He took my hand and kissed it. "You are her, aren't you? Madame Coumlie's successor."

"How did you guess?" The old guy had skin like

a well-worn saddle, cheekbones a model would kill for, and eyes as sharp and bright as a raven's. When he smiled, I noticed his teeth were worn almost to the gumline. His head was shaved and his bald pate was tattooed in an oddly geometric pattern of lines and shapes which nearly matched the mahogany tone of his skin. I liked him immediately.

"You are the spitting image of her as young woman." His voice was deep and mellow.

No lifeline, so whatever he was, he was one of mine. "You knew her?"

"I been coming to Shore Haven every summer for longer than I can even remember." He held up the palms of his hands and I recognized the rune symbol tattoos as nearly identical to Madame Coumlie's. "You might say me and Celeste travelled the same paths from time to time. Oh, the stories I could tell, you. She always made time to see what old Abe had turned up in his travels. I've got something for her in my trailer. I guess it rightly belongs to you, now. Come by after the park closes tomorrow night, and I'd be glad to give it to you."

"I'd be glad to." Easy enough to swing by after the viewing for Wiley Willy and Marjorie.

"It's a date, then." He gave me a wink, and then noticed Henri for the first time. "Well lookee here. What's your name, son?" He reached for Henri's hand and the two men embraced like old friends.

"It's Henri now. So glad to see you again, Sir."

Henri turned his head away from me, but not before I saw the gleam of tears in his eyes. Abe too, seemed overwhelmed for a moment as both men just stared at one another, each gripping the other's hand.

Abe spoke first, his voice suddenly full of emotion. "She would have been proud to see how well you turned out."

"Thank you, Sir."

For the first time, I saw how deeply Henri missed my great grandmother, and realized how much her absence must affect him. She had been everything to him.

Henri took a deep breath, and re-centered himself, a technique I recognized as one of Master Foo's. "By the way, Mattie. Abe here is just the person to ask about those dreamstriders you asked me about. He's been a lot of places and seen a lot of things. If anyone, other than Rhys, knows about them, he would."

"Dreamstriders?" Abe rubbed his hand across his bald pate.

"Yes. Someone who can enter dreams at will." I hoped he didn't notice my red face. "I want to know how to stop them."

"Doesn't ring a bell. Let me think on it and get back to you."

"No problem," I answered.

Something about Abe made me feel like he would have the answers I was looking for. I hoped so. I wasn't sure I could hold Luçien off for much longer.

CHAPTER 11

THE VIEWING FOR Marjorie Parry and her son William was held at Orpheus & Sons Funeral Parlor and Crematorium, a modest-looking yellow brick building located two blocks past the meat-packing plant in the Germantown district of Shore Haven.

The law was unforgiving with regards to vampires. No human bites without a contract in writing. Any violation, and the hunters were called in and the vamp was staked. No excuses, no second chances. In spite of Juno Rockover's assurances that the Hand of Fate was off the menu in vampire circles, I felt uneasy coming alone. I asked Lou to come with me, but he was on a stakeout for a paying customer, and Henri was too wrapped up in his man-crush on Juno and the band, so I was on my own. At Henri's suggestion, I'd sent Blix across the ether to find out what the hell was going with Rhys on in Scotland, so I didn't even have my little yellow-eyed buddy as back-up.

The first thing I noticed when I walked into the viewing, was how few, um, live humans were in attendance. When Brunson said that Marjorie had a lot of vampire friends, he wasn't kidding, and the tall, sere woman who greeted me at the door was one of them.

"Mattie, welcome." Her hands were cold, her smile warm. "I'm Neldene. So glad you could come." She led me into the room, tucking my arm into her elbow. "Your great-grandmother Celeste and I were dear friends for decades. It was her fondest wish come true when you showed up."

The two coffins, both closed, were placed on pedestals in the middle of the room, each covered in a heavily-scented blanket of white lilies, tuberose, and jasmine. Unlike other visitations I'd attended, there were no chairs in the room, and visitors clustered in small groups while a harp, cello, and flute played sweetly in one corner.

She introduced me to her husband, Enrique, the owner of Orpheus & Sons, and he too, seemed genuinely pleased to see me.

"So glad you came, Miss Blackman. It's an honor to finally meet you." Enrique bowed over my hand. He was wearing an expensive-looking suit and two-toned shoes. "Were you and the deceased very close?"

"Actually, no. I only met Marjorie once..." My voice trailed off. Better not mention that I was the one who delivered the news that—well, just better not say anything. "Mayor Brunson asked me to come."

Neldene and Enrique exchanged a look. Enrique pressed his lips together. "Ah well, I guess we should have expected that."

"He's convinced we were the ones responsible for outing him as a paranormal in the election, doesn't he?" Neldene asked. "Please believe me, the vampire community would never do such a thing. You must tell him that. Marjorie knew, but he refused to listen to her. Perhaps he will listen to you. We love Jimmy. We would never hurt him."

Maybe I didn't know much about vampires, but both Neldene and Enrique seemed sincerely upset at the rift between them and the Mayor. "Marjorie said the same thing, but I think his mind is pretty well made up. He truly believes the vampires conspired against him and tried to force him out of the election."

"It wasn't us," Enrique said. "Let us prove it to you."

I followed them past the reception area and into a somewhat cramped office area lined with file cabinets and bookcases, and two small computer desks. Neldene slipped into the chair at one of the desks and double-clicked on the computer's wastebasket icon. She then selected a file and sat back to let me read it.

"This email was sent to a reporter at *The Democrat and Chronicle* from this computer, just before the election. It claims that the Mayor is an unregistered paranormal." She then double-clicked on another file. "And this one was sent t to *The Daily Register*, saying exactly the same thing. She opened four more emails, all addressed to reporters of various news media outlets in Monroe County, including the local news affiliate television station.

I looked at the signature, which was the same on all the emails. "Who is Harvey Heller?"

"Our son," Neldene answered. Her eyes brimmed with bloody tears. "I was mortal when he was conceived. My mother was the park's seamstress—she made costumes for all the performers, including Madame Coumlie. Eventually I took her place. Madame loved my work, and I made all her clothes for her until her death."

She clasped Enrique's hand. "I met Enrique when he came to work as a roustabout at the park. We fell in love, and were about to be married when Enrique was made a vampire. I loved him then, as I do now. Harvey was conceived shortly after the wedding."

"So, Harvey was a Dhampir?" I asked. "And used your computer to send those emails to the press? Why?"

"He was a selfish, spoiled child," Enrique said. "We tried to give him every advantage, but he never forgave me for making his mother a vampire after he was born."

"Nor me for allowing Enrique to turn me. Believe

me, we loved him the best we could, but he grew up a rebellious boy. Enrique even started up the mortuary business so that Harvey would have a stable home environment. We made it into a successful business, but Harvey would have none of it. He dropped out of high school to join the band and turned his back on everything we did."

"Although he came around often enough when he wanted money," Enrique added.

Both of them looked so miserable and upset, I don't think they could have faked it. "Why would he turn against Jim Brunson? What did he ever do to deserve that kind of treatment?"

"He was convinced that if Jimmy was elected, the band wouldn't be allowed to play at this year's Sprit Festival," Neldene answered. "He thought that William Parry being the Mayor's nephew would make it a conflict of interest. The band would lose out on the biggest gig of the year."

Enrique's expression turned grim. "So selfish. James Brunson is a good man. He didn't deserve it."

"We only found out he'd done this after the election was over," Neldene closed the files. "What Harvey didn't realize was that the band's contract had been set up by the previous administration, and signed well before the election. There was no conflict of interest."

"By then, it was too late. James was already

exposed, and forced to register as an Alternative Individual with the FBI, and he was convinced the vampire community had tried to sabotage his campaign." Enrique put his hand on his wife's shoulder. "Even though he won the election, Jimmy cut us out of his life completely. You must understand the dhampir community in Shore Haven is understandably small. They *are*, after all, our children. To lose even one hurts all of us. And now--."

I gasped as his meaning became clear. "Hells bells. Your son was Kid Harsh, wasn't he?"

"Yes," Neldene nodded. "All the band members in Wiley Willie and the Rogues were dhampir. When Harvey was found dead, the police said he'd been lying by the side of the road for weeks. We knew it wasn't true, but couldn't go to the authorities, and Jimmy wouldn't take our calls. And then the Ramone boy disappeared. And then they found William, and Edward's body was so badly burned, they just assumed he died in the fire. And now perhaps Jimmy will listen to you when you tell him that someone is hunting dhampir."

CHAPTER 12

AFTER PROMISING NELDENE and Enrique that I would speak to Mayor Brunson (although I could never imagine anyone calling him *Jimmy*), I drove over the amusement park. It was after midnight, and the park had already shut down for the night, but the cleaning crew was still around, and the familiar sound of Juno Rockover and the Rogues was already blasting across the park from the vicinity of the ballroom.

I found my way to the gypsy camp were the vendor trucks and RVs were parked in the back lot, near the trailer part where Wiley Willy's body had been found. The night was balmy, and most of the vendors were sitting outside their campers. I got the feeling that this crowd far preferred the night over the daylight.

Abe's trailer was easy enough to find—it was as big as a moving van, painted in bright colors and bold graphics like a lurid comic book in three dimensional letters:

LIGHTNER ENTERPRISES PRESENTS:
THE MOST AMAZING COLLECTION OF
UNNATURAL ARTIFACTS &
MYTHIC CREATURES
THE WORLD HAS EVER KNOWN!
MYSTERIES OF THE OCCULT!
MAGICAL ANTIQUITIES!
YOU WON'T BELIEVE YOUR EYES!
SATISFACTION GUARANTEED!!!

I found Abe seated outside his trailer in a rocking chair, telling stories to a group of spellbound adults, crouched around his feet like a bunch of little kids. He caught sight of me and nodded, telling the group there would be more stories tomorrow night. There was a round of applause, and several people came forward to shake his hand before returning to their own trailers. To my surprise, Henri was one of them.

Once again, I was struck by my own reaction to Abe Leightner. I couldn't help but think he might very well be the coolest person I'd ever met. Instinctively, I trusted him. This guy was the real deal.

"Glad you came, Mattie. I've had this thing for Madame Coumlie in my possession for far too long, and let me tell you, it *wants* to come to you. Hang on, I'll go get it."

He disappeared up the ramp into the back of the van, his body spry enough for a far younger man. There was a plush, if worn, oriental carpet spread out on the ground, and lanterns hung at each corner, bathing the campsite in a cheery glow. I followed Henri's lead and took a seat on the carpet, near Abe's rocking chair. A soft breeze off the lake and a couple of bug zappers kept the mosquitoes at bay.

Abe returned a moment later, carrying a wadded up brown paper bag. He settled himself into the rocker, with the crumpled package on his lap.

"Now before I give this to you, I need to tell you a few things. First of all, it belongs to you; or leastwise, your line. I don't know how or why it was taken, but I think that once you take possession of it, you will not be able to part with it, even if you wanted to. So there's a responsibility that comes with accepting this item, if it is what I think it is, and if it's what Madame Coumlie asked me to find."

By this time, I was pretty curious. "What is it?"

He gave me a stern look. "Listen to what I'm saying, young one. To me, it looks like one thing, but I'm betting that only you will see the true nature of this thing. And once you accept it, there is no going back. It will change you. It is the nature of these things."

As much as I instinctively liked Abe, I couldn't help but be a bit skeptical of this bit of showmanship. I mean, the guy made a living from hauling his sideshow from town to town and charging people money to look at jars of conjoined cat fetuses floating in formaldehyde.

"Understood." I reached for the package.

Henri put his hand on my arm. "Wait a second. Maybe you should think about this. Rhys says--."

"Hey, in case you haven't noticed Rhys isn't *here*." Irritation heated my words. "If this thing was something my great-grandmother wanted, then I'm sure it's something that it was something she needed. And Rhys is not the Hand of Fate, I am. It's my decision, not his or yours or anyone else's."

The shocked expression on Henri's face stopped me. Even Abe looked surprised. "I'm just getting tired of everyone saying that Rhys wouldn't do this or that. Well he's not here, now is he? I haven't heard from him, and he's not returning my calls or emails. He was only supposed to be gone two weeks, and it's been almost four. I don't think he's coming back."

"I didn't realize this was such a sensitive subject," Henri said.

"Sorry." I squeezed his fingers and felt a reassuring pressure in return.

"What I was *going* to say," Henri began. "Is that Rhys has taught me not to accept packages from strangers, no matter how friendly they may seem, without seeing what is inside first. Why don't you ask Abe to open the package before he hands it to you? Then you can decide if you want it or not."

Doh! I gave Henri a peck on the cheek. "That's good advice. Thank you." I took a deep breath. "And thank you, Abe for bringing me this item, whatever it is. Could you unwrap it and let me see what it is?"

The old guy grinned and turned the package over in his hands, pulling at the paper. "That's a good thought, son, but I don't think it will make much of a difference, once she sees it." He reached inside the bag drew out an oddly shaped bit of metal.

He held it in the lamplight, turning it so I could see. It was an old, really old, pair of shears, formed from a single piece of brownish metal. Just two wicked-sharp bronze blades joined at the handle. When he opened and shut the blades, the *whisk* of sharpened metal rang like the song of my soul.

They *called* to me.

"What is it," asked Henri.

"If they're what I think they are, these were owned by the very first Hand of Fate—used to cut the thread of life. They've been lost for centuries. Madame Coumlie had me looking for them for years, but last year, she thought she would need them, and gave me this mark." Abe pointed to a glowing rune on the pad of this thumb. "All this time searching, and it only glowed like this when I picked them up."

The blades were covered with more runes, many of them similar to those on Madame Coumlie's hands, and Abe's too. I took them from him, knowing beyond a doubt that they belonged to me.

The bronze metal warmed beneath my grip

and the runes began to glow. A moment later, the instrument glowed like molten lava, but to my hand, felt comfortably warm. Like liquid, the runes slid off the blades and onto my skin, melting into my palm. As I turned the object in my hands, the glow receded, and so too, did the shears.

My hand was empty.

"Where did it go?" I asked. I rubbed my palms together. The new rune markings on the skin of my left palm were raised, like scars. I had no doubt they were permanent.

"Ain't that sweet." Abe grinned. "Yup, they're yours alright. Now that they've been returned to their rightful owner, they'll come to your hand whenever you need them, just like the tarot cards."

I flexed my left hand and the shears appeared, just as real and solid as they'd been a moment ago. When I let go, they disappeared again. *So cool.*

Not that I planned to use them--lifelines were fragile things. I'd killed a man by snapping one between my fingers. "Um, what tarot cards?"

"She has a deck," Abe said. "Very old, made from hippo ivory. If you press them to your hands, they'll speak to you, just like they spoke to her."

I remembered the tarot deck of bone tiles he spoke of, currently wrapped in an old orange scarf and stored in a cardboard box at the back of my closet. "Good to know."

I flexed my hand again, and the runes flared. The ancient snips appeared in my hand again, as solid and real as anything. They were well-balanced and just the right heft. They felt good in my hand. I felt stronger, just holding them; as if I were suddenly more powerful. Maybe that's not the word—more confident. And the satisfaction I felt seemed to echo with Morta's approval as well. Something taken had been returned to its rightful owner and all was good again.

I had a hunch they'd put an end to my nightmare visits from Luçien in no time.

CHAPTER 13

THE HOUSE WAS eerily silent when I got home that night. I went up to bed and was out almost before my head hit the pillow.

Naked, he rubbed himself against me and again I couldn't stop him. The most I could do was roll from side to side, but somehow, he managed to tighten whatever invisible bonds held me and I was at his mercy. I tried to flex my hand, willing my scissors to appear, but I couldn't even manage that.

My eyes were sealed shut, as was my mouth. He teased at my nipples with his tongue and teeth, sucking and biting until I could feel that this was no dream —he was right there in the bed with me.

His mouth moved lower, and when I tried to clench my thighs together, he adjusted the bindings so that I was more fully open to him.

He pressed his mouth against me, and my body again betrayed me. Tears trickled down my cheek.

This was wrong. I hated this feeling of helplessness, but I could not ignore his relentless licking and teasing and probing. The irresistible tension began to build.

Stop it, please stop! I tried to scream, but only sounds I could make were moans. My mouth felt as if it had been sewn shut. How could this be happening?

'Yes, yes, that's it,' he thrust his fingers inside me. I tried to think of something else; anything to distract me from what he was doing. When I tried to concentrate on my breathing, like Master Foo taught me, he put his mouth on me again and—oh.

'Nooo!' I sobbed mutely as the climax shuddered through me.

He stopped, finally, and wiped his wet fingers across my face. Suddenly I could see again, although I was still tightly bound to the bed. 'I don't understand why you all fight me. You know you want it.'

'Touch me again, fucker and I'll kill you. I swear it.'

He merely looked amused. 'Next time, you'll be begging me for it. In the end, none of you ever resist for long. By the full moon, you'll be pregnant, and my sons will carry on as I have.' And then he was gone.

When I woke up, the bed and my skin was covered with torn spider webs.

I screamed for a very long time.

CHAPTER 14

IT WAS STILL dark when the FBI's paranormal agent Ted Roper showed up. But by that time, most of the spider webs had dissolved. I hadn't wanted to call Roper, and it didn't help that he'd been the one who initially tagged me for Wiley Willy's murder--there was no one else. He had a lot of experience with the paranormal.

To his credit, he went right to work and was able to gather up a few samples of the remaining threads for analysis, all the while looking as if he'd just eaten something that didn't agree with him.

"You say the front door was unlocked, but you're certain he didn't come in that way because the stairs creak so loudly." He nodded to the open bedroom window. "What about the window? Open or closed when you went to bed?" he asked.

I stood in the bedroom doorway, hanging onto Henri's arm like a life preserver, watching as Roper combed through my bedding with forceps, searching for strands of silk. I was still too freaked out to go inside. "Open, but he couldn't have gotten in that way. The sash is warped. It won't open more than a couple of inches."

Roper directed the bright beam of a flashlight onto the window sill for a better look. With the click of a button, it changed colors and he leaned in for a closer look. Then he asked Henri to come hold the light while he took photos.

From the relative safety of the doorway, I asked, "What do you see?"

He snapped a few pictures before answering. "You're not much of a housekeeper, that's for sure. This sill hasn't been dusted in a while."

"Hey, it was freshly painted two weeks ago," Henri protested. "I've been so busy painting, I haven't had a chance to do much housework."

"Interesting." Roper took the flashlight from Henri and switched the beam again, then handed it back to Henri to hold. He took a few more pictures. "Come over here, Mattie," he said.

I steeled myself and crossed to the window to take a look, certain he'd found something.

Roper pulled a pen out of his pocket and pointed to a few scratches in the dusty sill. "What do you see?"

My hopes fell. "There's no fingerprints. You don't believe me."

He gave me a hard look and held out the

flashlight to me. "Oh I believe you. I believe you so much, I want you to march right into the bathroom and look for any signs of a bite mark. Chances are it will be someplace he touched you. Someplace intimate, I think. Look carefully."

I stifled a scream. Lou had told me the coroner had found a bite mark on the inside of Wiley Willy's thigh, but I wasn't supposed to know about that. A feeling of utter revulsion surged through me.

I snatched the flashlight and ran to the bathroom to look. Sobbing hysterically, I flashed the black light across every square inch of my skin, obsessively looking for the slightest blemish.

A soft knock finally brought me out of it. "Come on out, Mattie." It was Roper. The hard edge in his voice had softened a bit. "If you haven't found it, it's not there."

I slipped my robe back on, belted it tightly, and blew my nose. I got a look at myself in the mirror, and nearly lost it again. My eyes were so puffy, I could hardly see; my face, a blotched and puffy mess. I looked like a victim.

That was something I never wanted to be again.

I took a couple of deep, cleansing breaths like Master Foo had taught me, inviting peace and serenity into my lungs as I exhaled all the fear and shame.

Nope, still felt terrible.

I opened the door and handed Roper back his

flashlight. "You know what it is."

He shook his head. "That's the thing. We don't know, exactly." I followed him back to the bedroom, where he began packing up his equipment.

"You know something, though. You asked about a bite mark." I wanted to shake him.

He closed up his toolkit and gave Henri and me a speculative look. "Tell you what. You tell me what I want to know and I'll tell you what I can about the Wiley Willy case."

I gave him a wary look. "What do you think I can tell you?"

"Before he left, Agent Porter showed me your test results. You're a null. No paranormal capabilities whatsoever, yet ever since I took this assignment, every time something hinky happens in this town, you're right in the middle of it. So I want to know about this Hand of Fate business and why a Picston meter maid is the guest of honor at the biggest paranormal gathering in the northeast."

I shrugged, glad I didn't need to lie to him. "It's no secret. Madame Coumlie was my great-grandmother. When she died, I inherited the title. Tell me why you asked about a bite mark."

"A venomous bite was found on William Parry's corpse. The coroner determined that the venom had been delivered before death, and that it contained a previously unknown neurotoxin—so powerful that it liquefied all the internal organs."

He raised his eyes to mine. "Those tracks on your window sill look similar to those we found on the floor of the room where we found William Parry's corpse. The crypto vet over at the zoo was of the opinion that they could have been made by a large spider; perhaps a member of the tarantula species. I'll have to compare the photos to be sure. The webbing here in your room leads me to suspect that if we'd gotten there earlier, we might have seen something ah, rather unusual."

"You're saying a spider did this?" I shuddered at the thought. "Look, I know the guy. His name is Luçien Bold. His aunt runs the dress shop."

He acted like he hadn't heard a word I said. "You haven't answered my question. What does the Hand of Fate have to do with the Spirit Festival?"

I sighed. He wasn't going to listen to me about Luçien until I told him. "You ever heard of the Moirai? The original three Fates?"

He rolled his eyes. "Well, yeah. The three Oracles. One could predict a birth, one could say how long a man would live, and one determined when you would die."

"Their names were Clothos, Lachesis, and Atropos, or Morta, if you prefer. Legends say Morta commanded the realm of the dead. If you believe the myth, I'm a direct descendent of Morta. So, Morta, the dead, spirits, Spirit Festival—get it? It sounds to me like you have a theory about what killed Wiley Willey. What is it?"

He snorted. "That's it? You're the long lost kin of some Roman deity and they've got you named as the queen of some new age spirit pride parade?"

I was trying very hard to be polite, but his attitude sucked. "You are waay out of line here, Roper, and pitifully ill-informed. Whether you believe the newspapers of the time or not, my great-grandmother saved the town of Shore Haven. Twice. Once from a serial predator, who some believed was a demon. No one knows for sure, but the fact is that the Hand of Fate stopped him. And once she stopped him, she sealed up that portal beneath Sentinel Hill that no one is supposed to know about but the FBI, and banished all the loose *djemons* who were plaguing the town. And *that* is when people in this town started celebrating her as the hero she was. I didn't know I was related to Celeste Coumlie until recently, and I didn't ask for the title when she died. Some people in this town cannot understand who or what she was, but for others, the Hand of Fate is someone who will protect and serve those who are afraid to approach traditional law enforcement. So yes, sometimes they'll talk to me where they might not talk to a hard-ass paranormal investigator from the FBI."

That little speech had given me back my confidence, and reminded me of who I was. Not Miss Fate or some homecoming princess, but Morta's Hand.

It felt good to remember that. "Now tell me what you think happened here."

"We had a lot of weres and shifters in New Orleans. Wolves, coyotes, dogs, cats—even bears, if you can believe it. I think this thing can change shape. If I were you, I'd start keeping your doors and windows locked at night."

"*A were-spider?*" The idea didn't feel right to me. "Luçien Bold came to me in my dreams as a human, not some disgusting spider. Anyway, it's not even a full moon."

"I didn't say it was a were, but I do think it is some sort of shifter. I'll send these samples to the lab and then we'll both know I was right. Meanwhile, I'll have a chat with your friend Mr. Bold, if that's his real name and ask him about his alibi tonight and when William Parry was killed. I'll let you know if anything pans out."

"Aren't you going to arrest him?" I couldn't believe what I was hearing. "There could be other victims. The woman who runs the dress shop--." I glared at him. "You don't believe me."

Roper made an exasperated sound. "What do you expect? You call me in the middle of the night to report a man you met once came here and molested you and threatened to rape you. I come all the way out here from Rochester, only to find that the front door wasn't locked and nothing was taken. And only *then* you tell me that it was a dream. You've got no marks or anything to indicate that you were bitten, and I can't find a shred of evidence that indicates *anyone* was here. I've got nothing to go on except scratches on a dusty window sill and a few strands of possibly ectoplasmic material dissolving in the blankets. That's not enough to make an arrest."

I choked down the lump in my throat. "What am I supposed to do? I can't just--." He was right, I *was* on the verge of hysteria. "I've got to sleep sometime."

He smirked at Henri. "If you're that scared, don't sleep alone."

Furious, I forced myself to keep my voice calm. "All right. At least take me with you when you go to speak to him."

"Absolutely not." He shouldered his kit and headed for the door.

"Wait. I, I could talk to Felicity for you. If he's molesting her, she might feel uncomfortable talking to a man."

"No civilians. Besides, don't you have a job or something to get to? He tapped his watch. It's nearly 7am."

He was right, but not for the reason he thought. "No, Mr. Smartypants. I've got the day off."

"Calling in sick after a bad dream? Tsk-tsk."

"No, that's not it."

"Then what? Is today free parking day or

something? Why aren't you going into work? Something better to do?"

"For your information, I'll be riding in the back of a shiny new Cadillac Convertible, waving to thousands of cheering fans at the Spirit Parade. Too bad you're going to miss it."

"Yeah, I'll be thinking of you when I execute the search warrant on your dream guy," he smirked, and was gone before I could think of a retort. If I hadn't been so scared of Luçien, I would never have called him. It wasn't worth the aggravation.

Guys like that just...*doh!*

CHAPTER 15

THE PARADE LINE-UP spot was at the parking lot behind the Skate-Mor, at the corner of Third and St. Joseph, normally a five-minute walk, but not today. Both sides of Third Street were already lined with people who had arrived early to get a good seat. I'd guess nearly half the people I saw were dressed in costumes—everything from archangels to druids, pagan priestesses to witches, yodas to yogis. A little girl dressed as a rainbow unicorn caught my eye—so cute. More than a few had no lifelines at all. Everybody looked like they were having fun.

It was like Halloween in the daytime.

Sometime during the previous night, more rainbow banners, decorated with silver glitter, had been strung between the lampposts. Several of the restaurants on Third Street had set up takeaway food carts along the sidewalk. The smell of gyros and deep-friend onion blossoms had my stomach growling.

I didn't realize that so many of the businesses would be closed for the parade. Even Dave's Killer Burgers was closed, and I couldn't remember the last time Mel closed for anything other than an ice storm. *Good for him.*

I rounded the corner of the Skate-Mor and yelped at the sight of the dozen or so immaculately restored classic cars lined up for the parade. Oh man, this was great! Even better than I'd imagined. I caught sight of Mayor Brunson climbing into the back of a classic maroon and black 1938 Ford Cabriolet and made a beeline for him, at the same time wondering what model I'd been assigned to. Growing up with a brother who had a passion for maintaining and restoring cars and motorcycles gave me a real appreciation for them as well, but I needed to give Brunson Enrique and Neldene's warning as soon as possible. If someone *was* hunting Dhampir's he could be next. I'd tried calling him earlier on his private line, but he hadn't returned my call and this wasn't the sort of information to leave in a voicemail message.

Before I could reach him, I felt a tap on my arm and a familiar voice. "There you are! Come on, Mattie. Here's your sash. I'll take you to your ride."

Lacey Lippman stood before me holding a clipboard, a heavy-looking plastic garbage bag, and an armful of rainbow-colored sashes. With her bleached-blonde hair, false eyelashes, and spray-on tan, she looked more like a television gameshow hostess than

Picston's Public Information Officer. Until last year, she was a parking control officer, just like me. She's one of those super-ambitious types who pretends to be your friend until you're no longer of any use to her. Then after she's promoted out of the department and stolen your then-boyfriend, she acts like she's the queen of look-at-me and goes out of her way to be nice as pie when you both know she's faking it.

I can't stand her. And it wasn't because she stole my now ex-boyfriend, at least not anymore. No, what added insult to injury was the fact that while I was again dressed in my city uniform and sensible shoes, she was wearing a hot-pink miniskirt and four-inch heels that made her legs look ridiculously long—and every guy that walked by gave her an appreciative look. I felt like a toad standing next to her.

"What are you doing here?"

She cocked her head and gave me a phony smile. "I'm on the float committee, silly. I'm here to make sure you get where you're supposed to go." She handed me another of the dreaded 'Miss Fate' rainbow sashes. "This way," she said, and strutted toward the lineup of antique cars.

I draped the sash over my shoulder and hurried to catch up. At least I'd be sitting down. No one would see it—they'd be too busy ogling the car. I had my eye on the green Jag at the end of the line.

But when she reached the Jag, she kept walking.

"Wait, isn't this one mine?"

She shook her head. "No, you're here, on the lead float." She pointed to the massive, gaudy platform looming behind a pair of girls in band uniforms, complete with silver pom-poms on their white boots, carrying a white banner stretched between them. In big, bold letters, the sign on the front of the float said:

50th ANNUAL INTERNATIONAL SPIRIT FESTIVAL
GRAND MARSHAL FLOAT - THE HAND OF FATE
MISS MATILDA BLACKMAN
AND HER COURT

No way.

The float was a five-level pyramid job, each tier a different rainbow hue, covered in brightly colored crepe paper flowers. Crudely drawn runic symbols, decorated each tier with suns, moons, pyramids, and palm prints. On each tier stood four high-school girls, each wearing a prom gown, elbow-length white gloves, and a rainbow sash emblazoned with the words 'Spirit Princess' in silver glitter. One girl, with spiky, turquoise-blue hair rushed up to me, cell phone in hand, and breathlessly asked if she could get her picture taken with the 'Queen'.

"Megan and the rest of the princesses are from different high schools around Monroe County," Lacey said. "Enzo thought they'd appeal to a younger audience. After all, the old Grand Marshal was well, so *old*. Aren't they just adorable?"

"Adorable," I agreed through gritted teeth while Megan snapped a selfie.

Lacey pointed to the top tier of the float, to where a massive purple throne sat, covered in blue glitter, flanked by a pair of matching costumed figures, each wearing a papier mache unicorn head. "*That's* where *you* sit."

The blush started from my toes. "You have *got* to be kidding."

She gave me an icy stare. "Now *everyone* will get to see who you *really* are." Her voice dripped with sarcasm. She laughed and shoved the garbage bag into my hand. "Don't forget to wave!"

I scanned the parking lot, looking for Enzo, but he had the megaphone out and was instructing all of us to take our places, we were moving out in two minutes. Already, the lead marching band was starting to play

My cheeks burned. This was a joke—the cruel kind like in high school when they nominate some unfortunate loser for homecoming queen. No one would have dared to do something like this to Madame Coumlie.

What did I expect? The Hand of Fate was dead, and this whole Spirit Festival was stupid, and so was I to have let myself get sucked into it. *What an idiot.*

Everything I touched had either died, disappeared, or burned up. Roper was right. It didn't mean anything to anyone anymore. With all the hype surrounding the Spirit Festival, I'd forgotten that. Only Celeste Coumlie could be the Hand of Fate. I was just Miss Fate. Too late to get out of it now.

One of the unicorn guys, Scott, scampered down from the top platform and offered to help me up to the throne. I handed him the big black garbage bag, which was filled with individually-wrapped pieces of salt-water taffy, and scrambled up the platforms as gracefully as possible. When I got to the throne atop the pyramid, the other unicorn guy, who said his name was Barry, helped me strap myself in before he took his place standing beside the throne.

I watched Enzo climb into the back seat of the little green jag, and a moment later, the float began to roll forward. The music began to blare out from beneath the throne, and the sounds of Norman Greenbaum's *Spirit in the Sky* began to blast out at ear-splitting volume. The Spirit Princesses and the unicorns began to dance. The throne began to vibrate. The float pulled out of the parking lot and began to roll down Third Street at a pace only slightly faster than standing still.

Oh hell. Might as well get it over with.

CHAPTER 16

WITH A PHONY smile on my face, I waved to the crowd while the two unicorn guys, Scott and Barry, danced like fiends beside my big purple throne. I'm not kidding, they were really good and their enthusiasm was contagious. The Spirit Princesses were far more reserved, preferring to wave to the spectators, all float princesses *do*.

I was the only one on the float with candy, and once the crowd realized it, they started cheering and waving at me. As soon as I started tossing out the taffy, the crowd went wild—the cheering even drowned out the music at times, which was on an endless loop of that one song. The view was also pretty cool, and before long, I stopped feeling sorry for myself and got into it.

With Barry and Scott by my side, we threw candy to the kids, to everyone who'd come in costume, and anyone in uniform; just about anyone who had a smile for us as we went by. I even threw taffy to a couple of the police officers I recognized on crowd duty.

Two hours later, when the float turned off Third and we headed toward the end point at the old ice house, I was almost sorry to see the parade come to an end.

As we cruised toward the parking lot, I spotted three sheriff's cars, the Coroner's van, and Ted Roper's olive green government vehicle parked beside the ice house, which was now festooned with yellow crime scene tape.

A deputy waved the parade away from the lot, directing us to the lot of the meat packing plant next door. I unfastened my seatbelt and slipped down the platform to the edge of the float, barely waiting until it came to a halt before jumping to the ground. I hit the ground running,

The ice house had been condemned years ago, and a cyclone fence topped with barbed wire encircled the property. Several NO TRESPASSING signs warned violators of legal prosecution should they enter the premises.

I was sweaty and out of breath by the time I reached the circle of law enforcement vehicles. Someone had cut through the rusted chain link fence which surrounded the building. Crime scene tape and a Sheriff's deputy stood between me and Agent Roper, who was standing in the shade of the building, having a word with Sheriff Reynolds and an older fellow.

The deputy stepped in front of me. "This is a

crime scene, Miss. You'll have to leave."

I ignored him, and waved at Roper, hoping to catch his eye.

Instead, Sheriff Reynolds saw me and strolled over, his face grim. "What are you doing here, Mattie?" His eyes drifted toward my chest. The corners of his mouth twitched. "Or should I say, Miss Fate?"

Doh! I whipped the stupid sash off and shoved it into the pocket of my culottes. "It's another body, isn't it?"

He jerked his head toward the parking lot next door, noting the tail-end of the parade. "I can't believe I'm going to do this."

To my surprise, he lifted up the yellow crime scene tape and beckoned me to accompany over to where Roper was speaking to an iron-haired fellow with black horn-rimmed glasses and mutton-shop sideburns. The men stopped speaking as we approached.

"This is Craig Ferrens, the Monroe County Coroner. And *this*," Reynolds sighed loudly. "Is the Hand of Fate, Mattie Blackman."

Roper made a face. "Oh geeze, Blackman. Somebody mentions your name, and here you are."

They were talking about me?

"The call came in as an anonymous tip," Ferrens said. "The body was dumped here. No clothing, no identification. "

Lou Scali must have made the call. He had

connections in the coroner's office; I hadn't realized it was the *coroner*.

"The caller said the Hand of Fate could read people's auras. He thought you might be able to tell us whether or not this one was human or not. It that true?"

"You mean you want to know if he was like Wiley Willy?"

Roper shot me a sharp look. "You know what he was?"

"A *dhampir*." I debated whether to tell him about the rest of the band being *dhampirs* too. No doubt Reynolds and Roper already knew. The body in the ice house, whoever it was, wasn't Mayor Brunson—he'd been in the parade.

Craig Ferrens nodded, wiping his glistening forehead with a handkerchief. "I found four bites in the groin area on this one, and he looks like the others. We want to know if he's human or not. It would save us some time."

Lou must've told him I could read a dhampir's life line. I wasn't sure if I could tell after a body had died, though. "I've never tried it on a dead guy before."

"We're trying to determine if we've got a serial killer on our hands," Sheriff Reynolds explained. "Agent Roper has already concluded we do, but I'm not convinced there's any real threat to the *human* population. Dr. Ferrens tells me it will take 48 hours for the test results, but if you can tell us now, we'll get a jump on it. Maybe save some lives."

Of course. If the victim was another *dhampir*, law enforcement wouldn't count the death as human. Easier to keep it quiet and out of the news until they found whatever it was that was killing them. "Let me see the body."

The entrance door had been pried off its hinges, the air inside as hot and dry as a convection oven. I couldn't help but think that the tin roof could bake just about anybody into jerky in no time.

Roper led the way to the naked body, which looked so very similar to Wiley Willy's. Like tanned hide, stretched paper-thin over bones. No spider webs. No smell of decay, but an incongruous scent lingered— something familiar. Sweat dripped into my eyes as I leaned over the corpse for a better look.

The distinctive blend of Brylcreem and Aqua Velva triggered a flash of recognition.

"Shit." I wiped my face on my sleeve.

"You recognize him." Roper wasn't asking.

A sick feeling twisted in my gut. I raised my eyes to meet Sheriff Reynolds. "It's Mel Moody."

"Ah, crap." The sheriff squinted at the face. "How can you be sure?"

I pointed to the tattoo on Mel's desiccated forearm. "That's an Indigo Diamond Piranha."

"Is he human or paranormal?" asked Roper.

"Human." The sheriff sighed and ran his hand

through his hair. "He owns Dave's Killer Burgers." He made a face. "Now that is a damn shame. I'm going to miss those double bacon chili cheeseburgers."

CHAPTER 17

I HUNG AROUND until they got Mel bagged up and loaded into the Coroner's van. Sheriff Reynolds and Ted Roper seemed to accept my identification of the body—and immediately expressed concern that whoever had been killing off *dhampirs* had changed his modus operandi and had moved up to humans. Pending the coroner's official findings, a serial killer was on the loose here in Shore Haven.

The why, what, how and who it was remained a mystery. Reynolds, I knew, would be looking for a human suspect, while Roper would no doubt be looking for a supernatural killer. Neither man was going to say much in front of me, but both were on the same page in terms of keeping the news quiet until the last possible moment, and both threatened to have me arrested for hampering the investigation if I spoke to the press before either of them made a statement. This being Wednesday, I wondered if they would keep the news under wraps until after the Festival was over, or release it sooner.

Either way, I wasn't invited to the party.

By the time Roper and Reynolds were done warning me off the case, all the parade participants were long gone. I'd missed my chance to warn Mayor Brunson about the dhampir hunter. I called and left him voice message, saying that I would stop by his office in the morning, then started walking toward home.

On a whim, I walked up to Dave's Killer Burgers. The note was still taped to the inside of the glass door:

CLOSED FOR THE PARADE 11am-3pm

I recognized Mel's handwriting, He was alive when he locked the door. Whatever killed him had sucked him dry and dumped him at the old ice house sometime between 11am and 1:30pm, when the coroner got the call. Whatever got him had to be close by.

Someone in the crowd, perhaps. It could have been anyone, I suppose, but Roper and Reynolds were both of the opinion that Mel had been killed elsewhere and dumped in the ice house. That meant that the murder probably took place somewhere between the restaurant and the ice house.

I looked up and down the street, wondering where he might've gone. Mel lived in Webster, a twenty-minute drive. Not worth the trip. Under normal circumstances, I would have expected him to take a nap in his office, as he often did. Or, maybe he'd decided to watch the parade, after all.

The lavender and black awning of Les Belles Jollies dress shop caught my eye. Felicity had scheduled my final fitting for tomorrow. I remembered the way Mel had spoken of her when he mentioned her shop, and wondered again if maybe he and the seamstress had a thing. She was right down the street.

The shop was closed for the parade and the rest of the day, like many of the smaller shops along Third Street. I peered through the window. The store lights were off, but through the drape leading to the workroom, the lights were on. Maybe she was working. Probably on my dress.

I debated knocking. She really wasn't Mel's type at all. It seemed far more likely that he'd fallen asleep in his office and been attacked there. And he'd been looking so tired lately. Come to think of it, Mel looked as exhausted as I felt. I shivered as I thought of Luçien Bold.

At the ice house, Roper had smugly informed me that he's already interviewed Felicity. She told him her nephew had returned to Rome the previous week. When I asked about the spider webs, he said they were still waiting on lab results. He was confident it would turn out to be a were-spider.

If Luçien had really gone back to Italy, he couldn't be a were-spider and couldn't have spun those webs in my room. But Luçien told me he was a *dreamstrider*.

Maybe he didn't need to physically access the victim's room. What if he could get to *anyone* through their dreams? And if he was only in their dreams, what about the spider webs? Those were real enough; even Ted Roper had seen them.

There would be one way to be sure, though. If Mel *had* been asleep in his office, and whatever bit him was some sort of were, there would be spider webs in Mel's office. The police hadn't yet sealed off the restaurant. It might be hours or even days before they got around to it. The webbing might be gone by then. Dissolved, like it had begun to do in my room.

It wouldn't hurt to look. I knew where Mel kept his spare key. If anybody saw me, I could just say I was there to feed the fish.

CHAPTER 18

THE KEY WAS hidden in a magnetized box stuck inside the fender of Mel's red and white 1969 Ford Fairlane 500—a two-door fastback with bucket seats. The car, which he'd named Priscilla, was only driven in the summer. He'd been meaning to have it restored and detailed for years. Now, that would never happen.

I went in through the service entrance and paused just outside his office to allow my vision to adjust to the gloom. To my right was the big refrigerated walk-in, to my left, the door to Mel's office.

I walked tentatively into the kitchen, still warm from the morning shift. Behind the service window, the grill had been scrubbed, and the broilers and food prep stations had been wiped down. Clean dishes had been stacked neatly in place, ready for the next shift. The pick-up station had also been wiped clean and the chili and soup warmers had been turned off. The place looked orderly and clean. He'd planned for this.

I returned to his office and after a moment's hesitation, opened the door.

There were no spider webs. No sign of anything suspicious. Just the usual clutter and the still-powerful scent of Brylcreem and Aqua Velva. In fact, the Aqua Velva bottle was still sitting out on his desk, as if he'd just given himself a fresh coat of the stuff before leaving. Maybe he had a date. Or not. Mel practically bathed in that stuff.

Nothing. So much for my great idea.

It hit me then. I was out of a job, as was everyone else who depended on Mel. Dave's Killer Burgers was an anchor for Shore Haven. It had the best food in town. Everyone, be they living or dead, came here. It was the hub of the community.

What would happen to Shore Haven without it? Probably get bulldozed to make room for a bank or bought out by a franchise and remodeled. No more 24-hour chili fries, no more jukebox music, and no more piranhas in the dining room.

I went to the walk-in and grabbed the bag of thawed shrimp for the fish. I didn't know if Mel had family living nearby, but the fish were his babies and he would want them taken care of. I climbed the ladder beside the tank and settled myself on one of the rungs, before dropping handfuls of shell-on shrimp into the tank. You couldn't just dump all the shrimp in at once—otherwise the fish would get over-stimulated and begin attacking each other. They swarmed in eagerly to eat.

I watched them for a while, my eyelids heavy. The hum of the filter was hypnotic. I laid my head on the edge of the tank and slept like the dead.

I woke up feeling more alert than I had in days. The clock said six am—sheesh. I'd slept right through the night. And no bad dreams of Lucien Bold. Maybe he was really gone, of maybe he couldn't find me here. Good to know.

The school of newly-orphaned piranhas hovered near the surface, their fishy little faces hopeful for more food.

"Sorry guys, that's all there was. I'll be back this afternoon." I closed the top of the tank and climbed down from the ladder. After pulling another bag of frozen shrimp from the freezer I placed it on the counter to thaw. Mel was my friend. Until someone stopped me, taking care of his fish was the least I could do.

I was covered in blue glitter from the float. I needed to get home and get cleaned up before I drove over to Picston to talk to Mayor Brunson. I locked the door behind me and pocketed the key.

I caught up with Mayor Brunson in the parking lot at Picston City Hall as he arrived for work on Thursday morning. I told him what Enrique and Neldene had told me about their son, Harvey, and how he'd been the one who'd sent the letters to the newspapers, trying to ruin Brunson's chances to win the election.

"They feel terrible about it, and even worse that you won't let them explain. They said they love you and miss you. I believe them."

Brunson scoffed. "That's ridiculous. I don't know any vampires."

"We both know that's not true. You're a dhampir, just like Willy and the rest of the Rogues."

Brunson's jaw dropped.

"Don't deny it, I see it in your aura. I understand why you'd want to keep that out of the press, but Enrique and Neldene are worried about you. They asked me to warn you."

Brunson looked like he'd just been sucker-punched. "If this gets out, I'm through."

"If it gets out, it won't come from either the vamps or me. Look, you need to know that someone is hunting dhampirs. Harvey, er, Kid Harsh was the first to die—then Buddy Ramone disappeared. Then your cousin William and the sax player, Eddie Reale."

Brunson rubbed his mouth. "I had no idea. I thought they were being recruited to become vampires. Juno had been part of their crowd in high school, but he decided to turn vamp a few years ago. I was worried he was trying to convince William and the rest of the band to turn vamp as well. It's why I hired Lou. Then, when Lou found William dead, I didn't know what to think. The coroner assured me it wasn't a vamp bite. Some sort of venom, he said."

I didn't know how much he'd been told, but I wanted him to have as much information as possible. "The FBI special investigator told me he thinks the killer may be some sort of shape shifter or were."

"What, like a were-snake?" He gave me a doubtful look. "Full moon isn't until Saturday. Look, I saw you talking to Sheriff Reynolds and the coroner yesterday, after the parade. I saw all the crime scene tape. That was another murder, wasn't it?"

"Yes, but it wasn't a dhampir. They're trying to figure out if they've got a serial killer on their hands. Whoever or whatever it is, yesterday's victim was human. Mel Moody."

His eyes widened in genuine surprise. "Killer Dave?"

"Yeah. They're trying to keep it quiet until after the festival. Don't want to scare off the tourists or create an international incident."

"Oh dear. I suppose someone should tell Felicity."

"Felicity? Why would she know?"

She's the chairwoman of this year's Spirit Ball. Enzo told me that Killer Dave's was providing the food for the event. This is really going to hurt her plans. She looked positively exhausted when I saw her last." He pulled out his cell phone. "I'll have Enzo call her."

Secretly, I'd been positive there was something going on between Felicity and Mel, so maybe their relationship was purely business after all. It dawned on me that it might be possible to ask Felicity some carefully couched questions about Luçien. "Really? I'm having my final fitting with her this afternoon."

Brunson gave me pensive look and winced. "No offense, Mattie, but you're not the most tactful person. Better let Enzo handle it." He turned to make the call.

"No, wait." I stopped him. "What about you? I mean, have you met anyone unusual lately or seen anything that struck you as strange? Any um, odd dreams?" I had to admit, Brunson looked clear-eyed and on his game this morning. No dark circles under his eyes. His shirt and suit were crisply pressed, he looked as if he'd just stepped out of a fashion magazine. "Aren't you worried?"

"What?"

"If someone's hunting dhampirs, maybe you should be careful."

He gave me a sharp look. "I'm more worried that someone will let what I am slip to the press than I am of being turned into beef jerky."

I blushed. "No, I would never say anything. You have my word on that. Believe me, I know how to keep a secret. Enrique and Neldene wanted me to warn you, that's all. We don't know who this killer is. Until yesterday, I thought he was hunting dhampirs, but after we found Mel, it's clear that no one is safe."

"Well, thanks for the warning, but I'm not too worried. You see, that's one of the reasons why I live in Picston. I admit, I 'd rather live in Shore Haven, but here's a lot less of this kind of nonsense there."

I watched him cross the parking lot and disappear inside the building. He was right, of course; I'd never really thought about it. All the band members lived in Shore Haven. Technically, Mel had a house in Webster, but he practically lived at the restaurant. Except for his recent Spirit Festival appearances, Jim Brunson spent his days behind the secured premises of Picston City Hall, and his nights in his townhouse in gated community in a pricey Picston neighborhood.

There were no hotels in Shore Haven. That probably meant that the killer wasn't just here for the Spirit Festival. And Kid Harsh had died several weeks before the festival. That meant that the killer probably lived here. *Yes*. That sounded right. But Mel didn't. And Mel wasn't into music, and he wasn't a dhampir. In a flash of understanding, I realized that the victims *did* have something in common—they were all involved with the planning of the Spirit Ball. Wiley Willy and the Rogues. Mel Moody. Holy crapoli, that was it. I wondered if there were other victims that Roper and Reynolds knew about.

Probably. Only one way to know for sure. As much as I hated the thought, I needed to have another chat with Agent Roper.

CHAPTER 19

MY REDUCED HOURS meant I didn't work on Thursdays. That meant I had plenty of time to kill before my final fitting with Felicity, so I drove out over to the FBI office in downtown Rochester. The nondescript, five-story, 1980s government building was located near High Falls and the inner loop. It was nearly midmorning by the time I found a place to park, passed through the security screen, and made my way to the general reception area on the third floor. I didn't have an appointment, but the receptionist said I could wait for him.

Thirty minutes later, I was given a visitor badge, and Ted Roper led me back to his office, which I immediately recognized as belonging to his predecessor, Frank Porter. I'd been here a couple times, during Porter's tenure, neither visit had been particularly pleasant. You might say that Roper's office held few clues to his personality; either that, or he had no personality. It was just as cramped and functional as I remembered, with gunmetal grey modular furniture, a single plastic guest chair, and a couple of framed certificates on the wall.

I told him my theory, about how all the victims had all been dhampirs and all lived in Shore Haven. "The killer has to be a local. Someone who lives in the area and is involved with the Spirit Festival."

Roper shook his head. "Hey, give us a little credit. We've already considered that angle. First of all, just about everyone in Shore Haven is involved with the festival, in one way or another. And you and the sheriff both confirmed that Moody wasn't a dhampir, so that doesn't fit. And Moody didn't live in Shore Haven. And the sax player, Eddie Reale didn't actually live in the house with the rest of the band. He'd had a fight with his girlfriend a couple days earlier and was just crashing there for a couple days."

I couldn't help but think there was more he wasn't telling me. "Yeah, but he was a dhampir, and unless there are more victims you haven't told me about, Mel is the only anomaly. I mean, he closed the restaurant—he never closes. He must've had a good reason. And the window of time between when he closed up the place and whenever the coroner got the call pretty much nails his death to a two or three-hour window. You said yourself the body was dumped there. The means the murderer had to know about the ice house. Chances are better than good that the murderer is a local."

"Are you guessing or do you know something?"

He had me there. "Hey, I'm just saying, Luçien Bold had been staying with his aunt for the summer. He could have--."

Roper cut me off. "Give it up. We double-checked the aunt's story. Flight to Rome from LaGuardia last Friday. Believe me, he's not the guy. Besides, we have already identified a person of interest. We've got him under 24-hour surveillance."

"Who is it," I asked, not expecting and answer, but unable to stop myself.

"I'm not going to tell you that," he smirked. "Let me just say that he's been on our radar for years. We believe he arrived a couple weeks before William Parry's body was found."

"So you're saying you think a guy from out of town did this but you don't have enough proof for a warrant."

" When he makes his move, we'll be ready for him."

I shook my head and left, knowing he was barking up the wrong tree. Ted Roper hadn't listened to a word I said. I didn't know whether Roper was dumb or arrogant.

Time to talk to Felicity Caprice about her nephew myself.

CHAPTER 20

I ARRIVED AT Felicity's dress shop at 2pm, but the shop was closed and locked up tight. Her lavender car was parked out front, so she couldn't have gone far. My appointment wasn't until four, so I had a couple hours to kill. Might was well go feed Mel's fish. I walked up the street to Dave's Killer Burgers. This time, and there was a bigger CLOSED sign on the front door and Mel's car was gone. No crime scene tape, though.

I let myself in. Mel's office door was open, and when I peeked inside, it looked different from the day before. The Aqua Velva bottle was gone and everything was neat and orderly. The safe was open and empty, and his red accounting ledger and checkbook were gone. Maybe Mel had family in the area after all.

I checked the walk-in and noted that all the fresh produce and about half of the meat were gone, too. Mel's kin would probably be back soon to finish the job.

After grabbing the bag of defrosted shrimp I went out to the dining room to feed the fish. But I soon discovered that whoever had been in to close up the place had turned off the filter, heater, and light over the tank. The fish were all clumped together at the bottom of the tank, looking decidedly unhappy. Poor fish. The water temperature had dropped to 68 degrees. If I hadn't come in when I did, they would have died within a day or two.

I turned the equipment back on and made a mental note to contact Sheriff Reynolds about getting hold of the family. These weren't just any dime store goldfish. Mel had a select list of clients he sold the babies to. No doubt someone would be interested in the adults, too. Or maybe a zoo somewhere...

I couldn't feed them. The water's oxygen levels had dropped, and the cold water had slowed the piranha's metabolism. Any food dropped in the water now would be ignored and just clog up the filters. I had plenty of time before my appointment with Felicity. Might as well wait for the tank to warm up and feed them before I left.

I perched on the ladder beside the tank, my hand trailing in the water, waiting for it to warm up, but that probably was just a good way to get bit. I crawled up onto the open tank cover, where I could see the water thermometer better. Once the water temperature reached 78 degrees, I could feed them and go.

The quiet hum of the aqua filter had me nodding in moments. The idea of a quick power nap sounded great, but it wasn't a very comfortable spot, and I didn't want to accidently roll off the cover and fall into the tank. Henri claimed his meditation practice was as refreshing as a nap. I decided to try a little of Master Foo's meditation practice, concentrating on my breathing.

I don't know how long I lay there. I wasn't asleep, exactly, but when the fish began grunting nervously below me, I was instantly awake. The water thermometer read 80 degrees. *Good.*

I tried to get up and couldn't move. Very, very bad.

Once again, I was spread-eagled wrapped in silk. This time, bound firmly to the lid of tank. From somewhere near my feet, Luçien chuckled and began to crawl up my body. "So glad you woke up early. I thought you were going to sleep through the whole thing." Something had happened to his hands. There were smears of silk emerging from his wrists, and his fingers had curved into hook-like structures which continued to wrap silk across my lower extremities.

My mouth had been sealed shut was well, and my screaming sounded no louder than the piranhas agitated grunting below me. Luçien was naked, a cruel smile played at his lips. Long black hairs had sprouted from his shoulders and back, and along his upper arms and legs. "Although I prefer passive women, it's so much more fun when they're scared. Tell me, Mattie. Are you scared? You won't be for long. Ask Felicity. Once you've had the best, nothing else will ever do."

This was no dream. Beneath me, the fish were frantic, grunting up a storm, caroming off the sides of the glass.

He'd bound my hands across my chest. There was no way I could hurt him with my shears. The more I struggled, the tighter the silk threads pulled, until I could barely breathe. My legs from the knee down were tightly bound in silk. His hooked hands caressed the inside of my bare thighs. I tried to buck him off, but I was too tightly bound to the lid of the tank. Once again, I was helpless to stop him.

There was no one to hear me. No one even knew I was here. Tears streamed from the corners of my eyes.

He laughed then, and I saw two long brown needle-like fangs emerge from behind his front teeth. Brown liquid drops emerged from the tips as he lowered his head to my groin.

On blind instinct, I wrenched my body sideways, toward the water. The lid of the tank suddenly flipped over and folded shut. Secured to the door by his silk, I was suspended less than six inches from the surface of the water, but Lucien dropped into the tank full of hungry, angry piranhas.

They went for the fleshy bits first.

From my vantage point, I had a too-close-for-comfort bird's-eye view of the carnage. The water churned like a washing machine full of bloody laundry, splattering me with bits of flesh and bloody foam. He was a small man. It didn't take long before the bones started to show through the carcass. As the fish fed, their frenzy gradually slowed and I began to wonder how I was going to get myself out of the tank. I don't know how long it took, but eventually they stopped feeding, and moved back into their little rock habitat.

I pulled my scissors into my hand and managed to snip through the silk across my chest a few threads at a time, freeing my arms. There was no way for me to open the lid—my weight held it shut. Ever-so-slowly, I carefully snipped at the silk bindings. There was nothing to hold on to-nothing to brace myself against. As I cut through most of the silk, the rest gradually gave way and I managed to slip into the water without making much of a splash.

Thankfully, the piranhas were tired and full, and kept to their familiar corner, grunting occasionally as I slowly folded the lid back and carefully heaved myself up and over the edge of the tank.

I dropped clumsily to the rubber mat below, alternately sobbing and shuddering convulsively for a time. White bits of flesh floated in the still-dirty water, but most of the soft tissue from the face, skull, torso, and inner organs were gone. Only the strangely inhuman bones remained on the bottom of the tank. There were far too many leg bones. I looked closely to be sure that yes, he *was* dead. A deep satisfaction flooded through me, taking the edge off the terror I thought might never leave me.

My clothes, or what was left of them, lay in shreds on the floor. There were dry towels in the linen closet and I helped myself to a pair of checkered cooks pants and chef's jacket, rolling up the too-long sleeves to above my elbows. I debated calling 911, but this was no longer an emergency. Luçien wasn't going anywhere.

The only message on my cell phone was from Abe, asking me to stop by when I could. I called both Roper and Sheriff Reynolds, but neither man answered. *Figures.* The way my luck with men was running, I wasn't surprised. I'd be damned if I was going to wait around for a man to call me *ever again*. I left them each a curt message to call me as soon as possible, and let myself out.

I walked to Felicity's dress shop. I was after 6 o'clock, and the place was locked up tight. Dang, I'd completely missed my fitting. Her car was gone, too. She was probably pretty mad at me.

I didn't believe for a minute that Luçien was her nephew, or that she'd taken him to the airport. She had to have been victimized by him as well, poor thing. No doubt she and her decorating committee were over at the amusement park right now, decorating the Grand Ballroom for Saturday's gala. She'd been terrorized long enough—the sooner she knew he wouldn't be back, the better.

CHAPTER 21

I HAD NO trouble spotting Felicity's hideous lavender Ford Taurus in the Heavenly Shores parking lot. I parked next to her, and flashed my Guest of Honor badge at the ticket booth, which enabled me to get into the part for free during Spirit Week. Not a bad deal.

Abe's tent was on the way, and on a whim, I decided to stop in and say hello. With a nod to Charlie Crimmer, I ducked inside. Abe saw me and waved me over. Today he wore a top hat, striped yellow and white pants, and spats.

He gave me a puzzled look. "What are you wearing, girl? You look like one of those food concessionaires."

I shook my head. "You wouldn't believe me if I told you. I wanted to thank you again for these." I flexed my hand briefly, still tickled to see the ancient scissors came into my hand. "They came in pretty handy today."

"Glad to be of service." His grin was contagious.

"I've got something to show you over here."

He took my hand and tucked it into the crook of his elbow. In spite of the humidity, his skin was as dry as ancient parchment. He walked with an odd gait—each leg pausing in mid-air like a heron stalking frogs.

"You asked me about a dreamstriders. I thought on it and thought on it, but I couldn't remember ever coming across that term before."

He led the way down a row of glass-fronted cases housing a portion of his amazing collection of arcane, occult, and just plain weird objects he'd gathered in his travels. He paused in front of one, and pulled out a small silver key from his waistcoat and unlocked a deep drawer beneath the display cabinet.

Inside the drawer were dozens of large glass pickle jars, each containing some sort of dead thing. He lifted up the biggest and held it up for me to see the contents, a large grey-and-cream colored tarantula. "This is *Theraphosa Hallucinor*, or, as it's sometimes known, a dream spider. A much-dreaded creature of myth. No adult has ever been captured alive. Their silk is the strongest known. When you asked me about a *dreamstrider*, it got me thinking. Could it have been a *dream spider*?"

The body of the hairy thing was as big as my hand, and the legs, if they'd been stretched out would have been as long as my forearm. Ugh. A shudder ran up my spine. "I'm not sure. Agent Roper thinks it's some sort of shifter, but I don't buy it."

Abe eyed the creature in the bottle. "Dream spiders are all male. Adults can affect a human-looking male glamour. They have scent glands on their legs here." He showed me a pale spot near the tip of each of the creature's legs. Once they mark a victim with their scent, they hunt them through their dreams at night and feed. Once bitten, their poison immobilizes their victims and liquefies their inner organs. They feed like all spiders do, by sucking out their victims juices, leaving only an empty shell behind."

As soon as he said the words, I remembered Luçien's long brown fangs and the way the silk oozed from his palms. Abe was right. My mouth went dry. "That's it then. That's what happened to the dhampirs and Mel." *And very nearly me as well.* "It doesn't matter now though, he's gone."

Abe stared at me as if I'd just struck him. "Gone? What do you mean, gone?"

"I mean dead."

He shook his head. "Dead how? According to the fellow I got this one from, once they've had their first feed after hatching, these things are near-impossible to kill."

"Well, piranhas do a pretty good job. Luçien Bold is never going bite anyone again. His dream-striding days are over."

Abe put down the specimen and stared into my

eyes, gripping me by both wrists. "Tell me true, Mattie girl. Did he come into your dreams?"

I nodded. "More like nightmares." I didn't mention the sex part.

"They mate with human women. Did he--?"

"What?" I wrested out of his grip, wiping imaginary webs off my body. "No! He-I, *hell no!* He tried, but I dumped him in the tank. *Oh god*—at least I'm pretty sure." I shook my head. "No. I *know* he didn't. He never got the chance." I held my hand over my mouth. People were staring at us. *Get a grip, Mattie.*

Abe nodded gravely. "Good. When he mates, he injects a small amount of his venom into her, and continues to mate and envenomate her repeatedly. The woman begins to take on the characteristics of a female spider. The Tarantella is extremely aggressive, clever, and dangerous. She must feed frequently while the eggs grow inside her. As the eggs mature, she spins a silken lair, choosing a site that will provide plenty of food for her hungry babies when they hatch. Once all her eggs have been laid, she seals the egg sac and stays nearby, guarding them and feeding off the local population as she grows ever larger. The male also stays nearby until the eggs begin to hatch. He's her final meal. The hatchlings are ravenous, and are known to consume entire villages before they disburse and wander off. The only way to stop them is to destroy the Tarantella and her nest before it hatches. "

That could have been me. "That's disgusting." My voice cracked. *Or Felicity.* My heart skipped beat. What if it was already too late?

The more I thought about it, the more certain I became. "Oh shit. The nest. It's in the *ballroom*."

I pulled out my phone and handed it to Abe. "Call 911," I said as I raced out of the tent. "Tell them there's been another murder—no, wait." I stopped in my tracks. The park was full of people. Another dead body wouldn't clear the park. Only one thing could do that. "Tell them it's a *fire!*"

CHAPTER 22

I RACED TOWARD the Grand Ballroom in the center of the park, dodging families with strollers, packs of teens, preoccupied lovers strolling hand-in-hand and the park's own mascots and visitors in bulky costumes. My eyes scanned the crowd, searching for a security guard. Heavenly Shores was an outdoor venue; I couldn't remember ever seeing any fire alarms, although there were loudspeakers mounted throughout the park.

I spied Charlie Crimmer having a smoke near the Tilt-a-Whirl and ran over to him. "I'm looking for Felicity Caprice. Have you seen her?"

He frowned, his craggy eyebrows knitting together across his brow. "You mean the decorator lady?" His leathery skin crinkled with his smile of recognition. "She's got a whole group of them whatcha call spirit princesses decorating over at the ballroom. Mighty pretty girls, too."

"Come on. We've got to get them out of there."

He must've heard the tension in my voice, because the old guy had me running to keep up with him, and the mere fact that he was in uniform seemed to clear a path through the crowd.

We reached the ballroom and I tried the door. "It's locked."

"Hold yer horses," he panted, as he fumbled with his keys. "It's only locked from the outside to keep the curious out. What's the problem?"

I pounded on the door, but no one answered. "Something's happened to them, I know it." I briefly explained that there was a nest of poisonous spiders in the building, and that the call to 911 had already been made."

"Got it," he held up the key and inserted it into the lock. Anxiously, I pulled the door open and paused in the doorway, waiting for my eyes to adjust to the gloom. "Oh!"

Silver banners hung from the twenty-foot black ceiling, twisted and gathered onto huge silver knots the looked like clouds in a night sky. The walls had been painted with a day-glow mural of planets and asteroids which seemed to stretch endlessly into space. In the center of the room a mirrored disco ball hung, reflecting the tiny blue lights strung across the ceiling, giving the room and out-of-this-world kind of glow.

"Purty, isn't it?" Charlie grinned in appreciation.

"They been workin' on it for days."

"Yeah, it's gorgeous," I said, and I wasn't kidding. "But where is everybody?"

He stepped inside and I was right behind him. The door slammed shut behind us and the room darkened, lit only by the tiny blue lights overhead.

"Hello?" I shouted. "Anybody here?"

Charlie found the wall switch and flicked the lights. Nothing happened. "Must be a blown fuse." He shook his head. "Park security here! We're clearing the building. *Now*."

Nothing stirred.

"Mebbe they left."

I pointed to a pile of purses stacked up on one of the folding tables. "I don't think so. Those girls wouldn't leave without their purses. I've got a bad feeling about this."

Charlie reached for the flashlight at his belt and turned it on. "Gimme a minute to reset that fuse box. Be right back."

He crossed the room to a door leading to the stairwell and I heard him descend the stairs. The ballroom itself wasn't completely dark. The room was gloomy, but still enough light from the little lights to see. I flipped the switches again, but still got nothing.

An anxious feeling settled over me. Time was ticking away, and the urge to do *something* rather than just stand there and wait for Charlie to turn on the lights seemed pretty cowardly.

I crossed the ballroom to the stage where the band had set up their equipment. It was darker here, and I couldn't see much. I found another light switch and flipped it up, but still nothing. Charlie should have found the fuse box by now.

"Charlie?" My voice seemed somehow muted by all the streamers and decoration. Maybe that was the problem. He probably couldn't hear me. I crossed the room and opened the door to the stairwell. It was black as ink in there.

"Charlie, answer me," I commanded. Goosebumps prickled along my arms. Charlie was one of mine, er, Morta's. If he could, he would have answered.

I tried the light switch just inside the stairwell and brilliant light flooded the space.

"Thanks," I shouted. My relief lasted only until I spied Charlie's silver cigarette lighter lying on the stairs leading to the second floor attic.

The metal was still warm.

Charlie! I raced up the first two flights without hesitation. Halfway up the third flight, the stairs and railing were covered with thin strands of spider web. The runes on my palms began to glow. I flexed my left hand, and the heft of the ancient shears felt reassuring. I set my jaw and scrambled up the last flight, leaving tatters of broken silk in my wake.

The stairs emerged directly in the attic—a room

made nearly featureless by being completely covered in silver-grey webbing. Hanging from the rafters in the center of the room by wrist-thick silken cables, a lumpy, purse-like sack was suspended two feet above the floor. There was movement within the sack. Bulges rose and fell along its sides and bottom.

If the eggs hadn't hatched yet, they looked like they would any day.

More silk-covered lumps lay on the ground beneath the egg case. I spotted a clump of turquoise hair and my worst fears were realized. I was too late. I cut away some of the webbing, expecting to find another leathery corpse, but it was Megan, the Spirit Princess from the float. Unconscious, but her lifeline glowed feebly and I felt a faint pulse. Alive! I tried to lift her, but she was dead weight—too heavy for me to pick up and carry. I had to get them all out—even if I had to drag them down four flights of stairs.

I jumped at the sudden sound of pounding on the ballroom door below me. I recognized Henri and Juno's voices calling my name. Thank goodness. They could help me get the kids out.

"Coming," I shouted, and turned toward the stairs.

And screamed. Standing between me and the stairs was a huge, hairy spider-thing as big as a Harley Davidson motorcycle.

And it had Felicity Caprice's face.

CHAPTER 23

"WHERE'S LUÇIEN," she demanded. Her whole body, except for her face had been transformed into the Tarantella form Abe had described, only she was much, much bigger. Her speech, although somewhat hampered by the three-inch brown fangs, was full of malice.

I took a step back and she moved with uncanny speed to put herself between me and her egg sack. When she reared up on her rear legs, her face was level with mine. *Big fucking spider*.

"What have you done with him?" Every word she spoke sent a fine spray of brown venom droplets into the air between us.

"He's dead."

Long black hairs, which might once have been eyebrows, bristled along her forehead. "I don't believe you."

"What's left of him is lying at the bottom of Mel's piranha tank."

She bared her fangs at me. "I was saving him for last. He was only good for one thing anyway, and I don't need him for *that* anymore. When, the ballroom doors are sealed Saturday night, my hatchlings will have more than enough for a feast."

I heard the sound of breaking class from downstairs.

I gripped the shears tightly in one hand and reached for Megan's silk-wrapped body. "That's never going to happen."

"We'll see about that." With a quick movement, she tossed a thick stream of silk over my head. It settled on my shoulders and instantly began to harden.

I cut the thread with my shears, but she kept tossing more and more sticky threads, faster than I could cut through them. She pulled the rope-like threads toward her, and I was forced to move with them or be pulled off my feet. Frantically I sliced away at the silk, but it was a losing battle. She was too quick.

I held my hand up, palm outward, the runes glowing with an eerie yellow light. "Stop! I am the Hand of Fate. I command you stop what you're doing this instant!"

I'm no demon," she hissed. She stopped tugging on the threads for a moment. "You have no power over me, witch. I've fed only on half-blooded vampires. I've broken no *human* laws. My children and I will live for centuries."

I shivered at the thought. I could hear people downstairs. I wanted to shout and tell them where I was, but I had a hunch that I'd never get the words out. I had to keep her talking. "What about Mel?"

She began crawling backwards toward her nest, dragging me with her. "He stopped into the shop. He had a picnic basket with him. I actually think he wanted to surprise me and take me to the parade. Instead, he walked in on Luçien and me...It was kind of a shame, really. Did you know he recommended me to the Spirit Festival Committee? And when those dhampirs came in for their fittings, well, I didn't even have to leave the shop. And pregnancy makes one so very hungry, you know."

I ran at her, the shears upraised, but she was so fast. She scrambled up the webbing, using the hooks at the tips of her legs to grip the silk, all the while using two of her middle legs to throw more sticky silken ropes at me. She managed to cover my scissor hand faster than I could cut the strands away.

I heard pounding footsteps on the stairs. "Up here!"

She was above me now, perched atop the egg case, pulling my scissor hand above my head. I turned my wrist and started beating my arms against the egg sac.

I could feel agitated movements within the nest.

She gave a little shriek and redoubled her efforts, dragging me up with her. I felt a sudden stabbing pain in my hand.

She'd bitten me.

CHAPTER 24

I SCREAMED AS the pains shot up my arm, leaving ice-cold numbness in its wake. I imagined the toxins at work, dissolving my flesh from the inside. I didn't know how long I had before the poison incapacitated me. Whatever I was going to do, I had to act fast.

My scissor hand was useless. She'd secured it to the side of the nest. I had no gun, no weapon. I patted the pockets of the chef's pants I was wearing and felt something.

Charlie Crimmer's Zippo lighter.

One handed, I flicked open the lid and thumbed the flint wheel. I held the beautiful golden flame aloft, where she couldn't help but see it.

She froze, hissing sputtering dark venom, "Put it out, put it out!"

I moved the flame to within inches of the egg case. "Cut me loose, bitch."

All the bristles on her body stood up in agitation. She looked truly ghastly, but made no move to cut me loose. Only the gentle stroking of one of her legs along one side of the egg case showed me how very distressed she was.

I heard the guys come pounding up the last flight of steps. "Stop," I shouted. I didn't want to be distracted. I could hear them, breathing hard, somewhere behind me, but she was so fast. I didn't even dare look and see who it was.

"Here's the deal, Felicity." I fought to keep my voice firm. "The guys here are going to remove all the bodies lying on the floor *and take them outside.* You make a move, I'll set the nest on fire." Without taking my eyes off her, I spoke to Henri and whoever else stood with him at the top of the stirs. "They've all been poisoned, but they're not dead yet. *Go go go.*"

I didn't dare shift my gaze off her for a minute. She hissed and gnashed her deadly fangs, but I could hear the guys removing the bodies the floor behind me.

She narrowed her eyes at me--all eight of them. Her face was beginning to change, too. "It's too late. You can't stop it now."

My scissor hand and arm had gone completely numb. The stinging burn of poison was creeping across my shoulders. In my other hand, the lighter was growing hotter every second.

I felt a firm hand on my back and a low voice in

my ear. "Everyone is safe." It was Roper. "It's your turn, Mattie. Let us take it from here."

"I can't. She's got my hand sown to the nest." My lips trembled. "Get out, Roper."

At that moment, a pair of hairy, hook-tipped spider legs perforated the grey silk wall of the nest, followed by a bearded face with four pair of black eyes.

"Oh shit."

CHAPTER 25

EVERYTHING HAPPENED AT once. Roper wrapped his arm around my waist and gave a tremendous yank. My hand pulled free, taking a big swatch of the nest with it. A writhing clump of hatchling spiders, as big as volleyballs tumbled out onto the silken floor below. Felicity darted forward, fangs bared.

I dropped the lighter.

With a whoosh, the silken threads ignited and the room erupted in flames. I fell backwards on top of Roper, and he dragged me to the stairwell with him. Together, we half-fell, half slid to the lower landing, where I smacked my head into the wall. I lay there, too dazed to move. My arm was useless. It no longer felt like it belonged to me. The silk wrapped around my scissor hand was on fire. Using my other hand, I pulled it to my chest instinctively, trying to smother the flames against my shirt. I heard Roper curse, then he threw his jacket over my head and hauled me over his shoulder and raced down the stairs and outside.

I hit the ground hard, the wind knocked out of me. People were screaming. Hitting me, kicking me—there was nothing I could do. I curled into a little ball.

The last thing I heard was Roper saying, "Let her burn."

CHAPTER 26

"THERE SHE IS, she's coming out of it," a familiar voice said.

"Wake up, Mattie," Henri said.

I opened my eyes. I was sitting on the wet grass of the amusement park, leaning up against the wheel of an ambulance. Henri and Juno were kneeling on one side of me, while on the other, a woman I didn't know pulled a needle out of my arm, swabbed the injection site with a cotton ball, and wrapped it in place with a strip of hot-pink tape. Next to her, I recognized the handsome local veterinarian Dr. Jensen.

"Thank you, Dr. Ibarra," he said. "Mattie here is the last of them." He turned and winked at me, his eyes blue enough to set any girl's heart aflutter. "Actually, you were already coming around when Dr. Ibarra here administered the antivenin. How you feeling?"

Experimentally, I shrugged my shoulders and looked down at my hands. Thanks to Morta's healing powers, I felt no pain. My skin looked unblemished except for a black stain covering my scissor-hand, running halfway to the elbow. The runes on my palm glowed faintly, letting me know the shears of fate were still there, and always would be. "Okay I guess."

"The discoloration is caused by venom and should fade in time," Dr. Ibarra said. "You're lucky. That chef's coat is made of flame retardant material." She smiled and I swear she batted her long dark lashes at Jensen as she shook her head. "It's amazing how fast this stuff works. Thank goodness you had enough spider antivenin on hand, Adam."

"The zoo has a venomous spider exhibit. I had no idea the funnel spider antivenin would be so effective."

"What about Charlie and the rest of the decorating committee? The princesses--."

"They'll be fine. They were not bitten as badly as you. More like a bee sting. It put them to sleep, but they would have woken up on their own in a few hours."

I breathed a sigh of relief. I was feeling better every minute, and as I took inventory, barely a scratch. I reached for my hair and stopped. "What the hell?"

"You might want to get that worked on," Juno said. "The girl that does my hair is fantastic."

"Yeah," added Henri. "Leilani did mine too, what do you think?"

There was something indefinable about the both of them that looked different—and it wasn't just the haircut. Juno was wearing one of Henri's gold earrings in his ear. And Henri looked good—better than I'd ever seen him before. A lot of the uncertainty and nervousness which had plagued him since he'd become a djenie had been replaced by a steady calmness. He looked relaxed and grounded. Not even Master Foo's teachings had taken him this far. It suddenly dawned on me that Henri and Juno were an item.

Well, okay then.

"I like it," I said, and I meant it. I was a little worried about the whole vampire-djenie thing, but now wasn't the time to get into it.

A sudden surge of panic shot through me. "What about the spiders?"

Henri nodded to the row of fire trucks parked nearby. Behind them, the Grand Ballroom was fully engulfed in flames. I scrambled to my feet. Firemen with hoses stood by at the ready, but no one was doing anything.

"They're letting it burn to the ground," Henri said. "Roper wants to make sure nothing survives."

"Oh great. Better call Fontaigne." I'd be blamed for destroying both a historical landmark and the venue for the Spirit Ball. Miss Fate strikes again. I reached for my phone, but then remembered I'd given it to Abe.

Henri laughed and threw his arm across my shoulders. "Not this time. You're a hero. You saved everybody. Come on, the sheriff asked me to let him know as soon as you came around."

It was still dark when we got home. Henri and the guys invited me to join them in the basement, but I told them I was wiped out. I went straight to bed and slept straight through to Saturday at noon, when Henri told me that Roper and Reynolds were downstairs waiting.

"Give me ten minutes," I said, and dashed for the bathroom.

I gasped when I looked in the mirror. My beautiful long black hair was a scorched and sooty mass that looked like something a plumber pulls out of clogged drain. Soot marks smudged my chin and cheeks, and dark circles, like skid marks, rimmed my bloodshot eyes. I'd lost one of the brown contact lenses I wore to hide the yellow irises I'd inherited when I became Morta's Hand. I looked like an alien from another world. I took out the other lens, but the effect was not improved.

Ugly. That was the only word for it. And there was nothing I could do about it. I remembered my first reaction to meeting Madame Coumlie and how strange and frightening horrible she looked. She had killed people, and as much as I hated to admit it, so had I.

More than once, I hadn't killed Mimsy, but her death was on my shoulders. And I didn't even feel bad about killing Felicity. That was not normal.

Take a good look, Mattie--this is who you really are. What goes around comes around.

Karma is a bitch.

I blinked back the tears of self-pity. There's no mercy in the cold light of a 100-watt light bulb. The choices I'd made when I agreed to be the Hand of Fate were right there for everyone to see. I had no idea the price I would have to pay would be my true self. Mattie Blackman was dead. I couldn't even recognize myself anymore. I turned away from the reflection, promising myself I wouldn't look in the mirror again.

In the shower, I hacked off the rest of my remaining hair with my hand shears. I wrapped myself in a towel and went into Henri's room to steal a pair of his shorts and a tee shirt. I *really* needed some new clothes.

Reynolds and Roper were in the parlor, with a third man I didn't recognize. Reynolds and the guy in the suit looking uncomfortably stiff on the old camelback sofa, while Roper stared out the front window at the kids playing across the street. Both looked relieved to see me, even as they stared like they've never seen me before. I guess the real me was a bit too much for them. Self-consciously, I ran my fingers through my still-wet hair, despairing how little was left. I lifted my chin and told myself I didn't care.

Reynolds introduced the third man as Assistant District Attorney David Redfern.

"Howya doing, Mattie?" Reynolds asked, while Roper cocked his head at me his gaze settling on my blackened hand.

When I'd found Roper the previous night and thanked him for saving my life, he hadn't said a word—just swept me up in a huge bear hug that just about cracked a rib, before stalking off to talk to the fire chief. Reynolds told me Roper had been the one who'd beat the fire out of me. He'd been certain I was already dead before we'd gotten out of the building.

"I'm good." I gave him a perky smile I didn't feel and held up my hand. "Doctor says this will fade in time. Doesn't even hurt."

Reynolds looked as if he wanted to say something, but thought the better of it. "Glad to hear it. We've just got a few details we need straighten out." He gestured to the portable tape recorder, sitting on the coffee table.

"Don't worry," Redfern chimed in. "You're not in trouble, Mattie. The Sheriff here and the FBI have both convinced me that your actions were pretty heroic. You save a great many lives. We're not going to be filing any charges against you. You have my word."

So I told them everything.

Well, not *everything*, exactly. But most of it. Not the part about Lou Scali or the part about Jim Brunson being a dhampir. Actually, I didn't even mention Brunson. Or the vampires. Or Kid Harsh and the feud. And not the part about having a key to Killer Dave's or the piranhas. No point in saying anything about any of that, really. I mean, a girl has gotta have *some* secrets.

And *definitely* not the horrible part about Luçien Bold and what he did to me or how he almost did that other thing that I didn't even want to think about and how the thought of him or *any* man ever touching me again made me feel like throwing up. Or how the water in the tank turned red as the piranhas swarmed over him and the feeling of savage joy that filled me as I was forced to watch them *tear him apart*. Or the feeling of satisfaction I got when I dropped the lighter and the flames raced across the spider webs and the baby spiders started screaming.

No. I would never tell anyone about any of those things. Besides, all they had to do was look at me and they'd see it in my face.

"After Abe Leightner called the 911 dispatch, he found Agent Roper's phone number in your directory and called him." Sheriff Reynolds explained "He said you'd been asking questions about spiders and thought there might be a possible tarantula infestation in the ballroom at the amusement park. Agent Roper got hold of me, and I called the zoo's crypto-vet and told him to bring every kind of antivenin he had. By the time I got there, the victims had already been removed from the building, and Roper had gone back for you. Five minutes later, the whole attic went up in flames, and Roper came out with you on fire, looking like he'd seen a ghost."

Roper gave me a wan smile, but said nothing.

Five hours later, we were done, and the whole time, Roper never said a word. The sun was heading toward the horizon by that time, so Henri and I went out to the front porch to watch the sunset. There was a package addressed to me lying on the old porch swing.

No return address. I looked at Henri, who was grinning like an idiot. "What's this?"

He shook his head. "I have been sworn to secrecy. Open it."

Inside, I found a handwritten note, taped to tissue paper:

> *Dear Mattie,*
> *Thank you so much for intervening with Jimmy on our behalf. All is well, and on behalf of Enrique and I, and the entire Orpheus community, you have our deepest gratitude.*
>
> *I've made the Hand of Fate's gala gown every year since the very beginning. After meeting you, I was inspired to make this small offering. If you haven't already purchased a*

dress for the gala, I hope this one will suffice.

With kind regards,
Neldene

I tore at the tissue paper, then gasped when I saw the shimmery silver fabric. Soft to the touch. It glimmered like eelskin. I lifted it out of the box by the shoulders, holding it up in front of me so Henri could see it too.

Sleek and sleeveless, the dress was cut like a tee-shirt with a simple ballet neckline and a slit on one side. Perfect.

I put it back in the box and covered it with tissue. "Too bad I can't wear this."

"Don't say that," Henri rose and took the box from me. "I gave her one of your bras and a pair of your panties, so it should fit perfect."

"*What?*" So *that's* where they disappeared to. "Henri, you can't just go around giving away people's underwear. Besides, it doesn't matter now, the Spirit Ball is cancelled. The ballroom is gone. Burned up. Phfft."

"They moved the location. They're holding it outside, along the lakeshore."

"I can't go. I can't—can't face all those people." I hated the whiny sound of my voice.

"Yes you can. The gala isn't like the other events

of Spirit Week. It's invitation only. For the supernatural community. No humans allowed. You're the Hand of Fate, Mattie. This is your night and you're going." The expression on his face was one I'd never seen before. Authoritative. Determined.

"It doesn't matter. I'm not going. I look..."

At that moment a battered black Subaru station wagon roared up to the front of the house. A young woman with shaggy purple hair got out and walked up to the porch, carrying a canvas satchel. She gave a little wave to Henri, and held out her hand to me, her eyes looking me up and down. Her smile was warm and genuine. "I'm Leilani. I'll be doing your hair and makeup."

They wouldn't take no for an answer. Leilani sat me down in the kitchen and proceeded to sort out the ruin of my hair for an hour. Tentatively, I touched the results, secretly horrified. There was hardly anything left at all.

"You have a beautiful skull," Leilani assured me.

She held up the mirror, but I couldn't bear to look. I turned my head away. "I know what I look like."

She took me upstairs to the bathroom to do my makeup. This time, she didn't ask about the mirror, and I was grateful.

At the bottom of the dress box, there was a pair of sandals with narrow straps that criss-crossed up my calves. I had to admit, they were pretty fabulous. And when Leilani slid Neldene's dress over my head and smoothed it down my body, I forgave Henri for giving away my undies. I could tell by the feel of it, the fit was perfect. I felt slim and sleek, and that was good enough.

Henri, looking very sharp in a tuxedo, knocked on the door to my room. He whistled when he saw me. "You look..." He shook his head, but he was smiling. "Amazing. Your escort is waiting downstairs."

A stab of panic surged through me. What was I thinking? "No. This was a mistake. I'm not going out there. I'm not going to go and make a fool of myself. Help me get this thing off," I said to Leilani. "I can't do this." I caught the horrified expression on Leilani's face. "I'm sorry."

Without a word, Henri took me by my elbow and steered me downstairs anyway.

I don't know what I was expecting, but when I saw Lou Scali standing in the parlor in a tux and tails, all the tension went out of me. Lou was a good guy.

I grinned in spite of myself. "Looking pretty sharp there, Lou."

He beamed at me. "You clean up pretty good yourself, Chili-fry." I hardly even flinched when he put the flower corsage around my blackened wrist.

Juno and the rest of the band had already left, so Henri and I squeezed into Lou's Subaru and headed over to the amusement park.

On the way, Lou confirmed he'd been the one who'd called in the tip about the body in the ice house. "I was parked in the parking lot next door, waiting for a client, and this car drove up with two people inside. It was too far away to see their faces or get a license plate. The passenger got out and lifted something out of the trunk wrapped in a tarp. He was a little guy, but he carried that thing as if it weighed nothing. He was in and out of the building less than two minutes. I was pretty sure it was another body, but I had no idea it was Mel. I'm sorry Mattie. I know he was a friend of yours."

"Yeah. I'm going to miss him."

"Me too."

CHAPTER 27

WE ARRIVED AT Heavenly Shores just before midnight. The authorities had closed the park after the fire, but the parking lot was packed with cars. Henri, Lou, and I walked beneath an arbor lit by tiny twinkle lights leading to the lakeshore.

I paused at the crest of the path, admiring the scene before me. Yellow lights had been strung around the trunks and through the branches every tree and light post along the shore. Overhead, the beautiful white moon cast silver reflections across every ripple on the lake. Someone had brought in truckloads of clean sand to widen the beach , and hundreds of people were dancing barefoot to the rockin' sockin' sounds of Juno Rockover and the New Rogues. As I gazed out over the happy group, I even caught sight of demon or two, and several creatures that were obviously not mortals of this plane.

It hit me then that all of the costumes I'd seen throughout the week might not have been worn by humans in cosplay. *No shit.*

I leaned over and gave Henri a peck on the cheek. "Thank you," I whispered. "For making me come. For everything."

"Thank goodness you're here," a voice from behind me said. "And your timing is perfect." It was Neldene, dressed in midnight blue sequins, flanked by Enrique and Mayor Jim Brunson, both in white tie.

Brunson grinned. "Wouldn't be a proper Spirit Ball without you, Mattie."

Enrique took my hand and raised it to his lips. "You look very beautiful tonight."

Yeah, right.

A sudden spotlight hit the four of us, and the band stopped playing. Everyone turned to look at us.

My heart pounded, and I reached for my hair, but with the spotlight on us, there was nowhere to hide.

"Don't worry," Neldene whispered, "Everyone knows what happened. You're a hero, Mattie."

Enrique led the way down the gentle slope to the lakeshore, and with both Neldene and Mayor Brunson behind me, I had no choice but to follow. As we approached the silent crowd, people on either side moved back, opening a path to the stage. I saw a few faces I recognized, like Charlie Crimmer and Mimsy's mother, Mrs. Wu. Everyone was smiling at me, and as we passed through the audience, someone started to clap.

The applause moved through the crowd like a wave, growing louder was we approached the stage. I bit my lips to hold back the tears. The cheering started as Enrique helped me up the steps to the microphone. There were even a few were-wolf howls. Everyone laughed, but it was okay.

Enrique gave a short speech of welcome and went on to describe the passing of Celeste Coumlie and about how wonderful it was to embrace the new Hand of Fate outside under the full moon, just like they'd done in the old days. There was some embarrassing stuff in there about single-handedly destroying the dream spiders and saving lives, but that was about it.

Then Megan, the girl with the turquoise blue hair from the float, who'd been pulled out of the spider lair by Juno and Henri, came up and presented me with a beautiful bouquet of dark pink roses. I pretty much lost it right there.

Enrique motioned me to the microphone, and asked me to say a few words I managed to mumble my thanks for the warm welcome, but that was all I had. Fortunately, Juno and the gang were right there, and the music started right back up. I was free.

I spent the next ten minutes wading through the crowd, accepting congratulations from strangers, and looking for a bathroom. When I finally found it, the women in line all applauded, told me I looked great, and insisted I move to the front of the line. They applauded even louder when I flushed the toilet.

Yeah, good times.

The band was really building up a head of steam, and everyone was having too much fun to pay much attention to me. With the pressure off, I headed toward the food table, wondering what kind of appetizers they might be serving.

A man stepped into the path in front of me. His green eyes glittered in that special way that always made my heart beat faster.

"Hello, beautiful."

Rhys.

THE END

ABOUT THE AUTHOR

Award-winning author Sharon Joss writes science fiction, fantasy and horror. She is the author of six novels, including *Aurum*, *Brothers of the Fang*, and the alternate history thriller, *Steam Dogs*. In 2015, she won the Writers of the Future Golden Pen award for speculative fiction with her novella, *Stars That Make Dark Heaven Light*. She lives amid a thicket of blackberry vines in Oregon and writes full-time. Find out more about her and her books by going to www.sharonjoss.com

AUTHOR'S NOTE

Thank you for giving this book a read. If you enjoyed it, please tell your friends and consider leaving a review on Amazon or Goodreads, even if it's only a line or two; it would make all the difference and would be very much appreciated.

If you'd like a quick note when I have a new release, please sign up for my new release mailing list at:

http://bit.ly/1MhS3lb

Your email will never be shared and you can unsubscribe at any time. I'll send you a free e-book right away and occasionally send out information about contests or opportunities to snag review copies).

OTHER GREAT TITLES BY SHARON JOSS

SOME PEOPLE ATTRACT STRAY CATS.
WITH MATTIE BLACKMAN, IT'S DEMONS.

At work, in her car, even at the foot of her bed. And with the FBI on the hunt for a rogue demon master, she's desperate to get rid of them. Thwarted at every turn to solve her problem through legitimate channels, she turns to Shore Haven's sexy mage for the answer: a fate she refuses to accept.

But as the serial killer's victims pile up, Mattie realizes there's only one way to stop a demon master. To save her friends and the people she loves, Mattie must choose between her life and her destiny.

ZOMBIES, WIZARDS, & DRAGONS

Mattie Blackman is the last living descendent of the Goddess Morta. As the new Hand of Fate, she discovers her powers over the undead can't help solve her problems with the living. When Shore Haven's supernatural community is threatened and one of her friends murdered, Mattie is accused and must solve the mystery on her own. This time, she and her demon Blix face a vodoun sorcerer with powers more dangerous than death itself--and he wants nothing less than her immortal soul.

OTHER GREAT TITLES BY SHARON JOSS

Winner of the
2015 GOLDEN PEN AWARD

Worlds and species collide on the planet Hesperidee in this classic winning tale of love, duty, and the future of humanity.

"STARS THAT MAKE DARK HEAVEN LIGHT is an amazing story, as powerful as it is beautiful. Award-winning author Sharon Joss manages to prove herself to be one of the best writers of our time."
*--New York Times bestselling author
David Farland*

DETECTIVE MIKE BANE is a shape shifter with two beasts: a 300-lb black jaguar with a taste for turtle meat, and a psychotic Olmec shaman named Tehuantl with a taste for blood.

When Mike accepts a security job at Mythica, America's only supernatural theme park, he discovers an unexpected kinship with the park's werewolf pack. But when his curiosity gets the best of him, he's ensnared in a centuries-old feud between Mythica's vampires and the fae of the neighboring

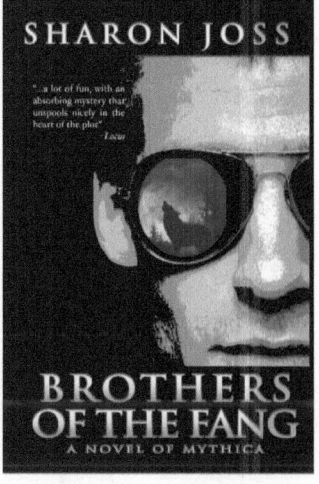

High Tor clan. Only Tehuantl's magic can save Mike's brothers of the fang; in return, Tehuantl wants permanent possession of Mike's body, mind, and soul.

Look for the next volume in the Hand of Fate series:

COMING IN 2016